RAINBOW'S END

A Swamp Yankee Mystery

BOOK THREE

JAMES Y. BARTLETT

This book is a work of fiction. Names, characters, businesses, organizations, places, events and incidents either are the product of the author's imagination or are used fictitiously. Any resemblance to actual persons, living or dead, events, or locales is entirely coincidental.

For information contact;

Yeoman House Books
10 Old Bulgarmarsh Road
Tiverton, RI 02878

www.jamesybartlett.com

Cover design by Todd Fitz of Fuel Media

ISBN:978-1-7363930-6-2

First Edition: September 2022

Second Edition: March 2026

10 9 8 7 6 5 4 3 2 1

For Susan

We're after that same rainbow's end
Waitin' round the bend,
My Huckleberry friend,
Moon River, and me

—*Johnny Mercer*

CHAPTER 1

Gus Haddock was up, dressed and halfway into his morning five-mile run. It was the middle of June and the sun, even at a little after six a.m., was already climbing high in the east and had painted the Sakonnet River--which Gus could see now and then off to the left as he ran--a bright and cheerful blue. Gus ran almost every day, both to keep up his fighting trim, even though it had been more than a year since he resigned from his U.S. Army Rangers squadron in the Middle East, and to reduce some of the stress he felt now that he was chief of police in Little Penwick, Rhode Island, the smallest town in the smallest state in the Union.

He wore navy running shorts and a green Rangers T-shirt and the only indication that he was the chief of police was the radio unit he wore--the receiver unit clipped onto the elastic band on his shorts and the handset unit flopping around on his back, pinned to the collar of his T-shirt. In the year and change he had been chief of police here in his hometown, his morning runs had never been interrupted by a call on the radio from Dottie Adams in dispatch. But as a Ranger, Gus Haddock had been drilled in the importance of being prepared, so he carried his rig with him as he ran.

His five-mile run took him roughly forty-five minutes at an easy pace. He didn't have a time he had to beat, as he had in the Rangers, so he set an easy pace on the mostly flat roads that skirted along the broad tidal river that didn't so much flow into the Atlantic Ocean as simply existed as an extension of it. At this time of day, when the seagulls were just beginning their daily search for food among the rocks and beaches, there weren't any humans about. Which was another reason why Gus liked to run early in the mornings. It was quiet, it was peaceful and nobody was asking Gus Haddock to solve their problems. Unlike the rest of the day.

The pace of life in Little Penwick had picked up since the Memorial Day weekend signaled the beginning of the summer season. That meant the population of the small town was expanded by three or four thousand new residents as the Summer Trade came back to open their beach cottages and mansions, sweeping out the winter dust and cobwebs, washing down the windows and decks, putting out the cushions on the Adirondack chairs, making sure the propane tanks on the grill were refilled and getting the golf clubs and tennis rackets out of storage, ready for a brand new season of fun in the sun.

It had only been a few weeks since Memorial Day, but Gus had already noted a slight uptick in the number of cases of DUI. That happened every year, too, as the summer trade residents came to town thinking that now they were temporarily living in a new town, that they could do anything they wanted and get away with it. This happened every year, until Chief Haddock's small police department had cited four or five drivers for being under the influence. Once the word got out that the local cops were enforcing the drunk driving laws, especially near the usual places like the Roadhouse restaurant and bar, the country club late at night and the dining club down at Penwick Point, the summer trade would pull themselves together and behave. For the most part.

Although Gus Haddock went running to relieve his stress and tension, he couldn't help thinking about some of his current problems at the police department. He needed to start the process of recruiting and hiring two new officers. Two of his officers, Carl Lincoln and Jamie McMaster, had told Gus they were moving on at the end of summer.

McMaster had been hired to join the force in Fall River, a small and grimy mill city on the Taunton River just across the Massachusetts state line to the north. Gus understood: the Little Penwick Police Department was a good stepping stone, a first job for someone looking for a career in law enforcement. A good next step would be a few years working in Fall River, where the population was larger and the ethnic make-up much different, so that the amount and types of crimes were much different from rural and bucolic Little Penwick. Officers working in Fall River with its more diverse ethnic make-up, would have regular encounters with violent crime, domestic abuse, car theft, vandalism and graffiti and more. And with a larger, denser population came more automobile crashes, emergency medical calls and other demands for police responses that kept someone busy throughout the shift.

Carl Lincoln, his other departing officer, was going back to school. He wanted to get his Masters degree in law enforcement, which would put him in position to hire on to a new police force as a commanding officer or a detective. He was probably looking to join the Providence department, which was large enough and funded enough to be able to hire all kinds of upper level staff.

Gus reached the tall Indian Post rock sitting just off the road, which was his turn-around point. The reddish basalt monolith, left behind millenia ago when the seas receded and the land was riven with volcanic eruptions and covered in glacial ice, had probably been called the Indian Trading Post Rock by the early settlers in this area. It made sense that the newcomers wanted to trade with the indigenous people -- here the Wampanoag tribe -- and they likely agreed to meet at the tall red rock near the river. Hence, the Indian Trading Post Rock, which, over time, was shortened into the Indian Post Rock.

Once he reached the rock, he turned and headed back the way he had just come. Gus picked up his pace aiming to do the last two and a half miles in a little more than fourteen minutes. He was running on the Indian Hill Road which was a quiet street of large homes and farms. There had been only a few cars overtaking him during his run, so he could stay in the middle of the road.

One of those cars had approached him from the south, the direction he was now running, so he saw it coming and veered over to the verge of the road. He gave the car a brief wave as it passed. He put his head down and concentrated on keeping his speed at a steady pace, increasing it slightly when he crested a hill and started down the other side.

He was making good time, legs pumping, breathing hold-ing steady, feeling strong. Which is why he didn't notice the car coming up on him from behind. Until some primordial part of his brain heard the slight acceleration, or the soft squeal of the tires on the pavement, or maybe felt the vacuum of air sucked away by the approach of the three thousand pound collection of metal and glass and plastic, doing about forty on the empty road.

Whatever it was, it triggered a response in Gus' brain and somehow he managed to glance quickly over his shoulder to see the bumper and left panel of the car bearing down at him. He leaped sideways and twisted and managed to avoid, at the last possible second, the front edge of the car. The driver's side mirror caught him on the upper arm and send him flying off the road and into a shallow ditch built to siphon off rainwater from the road. He fell, hard, against the wall of the ditch, tak-ing the brunt of it on his ribcage. The force of the fall knocked all the wind out of his lungs.

He lay there in the ditch, tall grasses tickling his face, stunned, for several minutes. He was not sure how long. He quickly began gasping for air to replace that which had been forced out of his lungs, and when he could breathe again, he rolled over, back against the ditch wall and took inventory.

His ribs ached. He suspected one or two might be broken. His left arm hurt where the mirror had struck it, but Gus didn't think it was broken. His left knee, on the other hand, was sending out frantic bulletins of pain. Gus looked down and saw a dark gray rock resting on the bottom of the ditch and knew that his knee had collided with it. He began moving his other limbs and rolled his neck and decided nothing else was broken. He felt like he had been run over by a truck, but he knew he had been extremely lucky to have evaded the worst of what might have happened to him.

He reached for his radio handset, and only then did he realize it was not clipped to his running clothes anymore. He glanced around and finally saw the black plastic of the handset part, smashed into several pieces. He couldn't move his head around enough to see where the radio receiver unit had gone. With the force of his tumble, it could have flown off anywhere.

It was several minutes before he could ignore the spasms of pain in his knee and ribs to gingerly stand upright. The car that had tried to run into him was long gone. Indian Hill Road was empty, blissfully quiet in the warm June morning, sunlight dappling the surface of the street. Birds were singing in the trees overhead, blissfully unaware of the man in the ditch.

Gus Haddock gathered himself and began walking ... limping ... back towards his home.

CHAPTER 2

It was nearly ten o'clock before Gus limped into the Little Penwick Police Station in the Public Service complex. His knee was swollen to about twice its normal size, every breath he took was painful and the right side of his face was bruised and scratched.

Ken Purcival, the officer on duty at the front desk, took one look at his chief and rose from his chair and came through the door from the squad room to help.

"Geez, chief," he said, "What the hell happened to you?"

"Attacked by a car," Gus said wryly, limping towards his office. "While I was running this morning."

"You get the plates?" Purcival said.

Gus shook his head, then stifled a groan. Shaking his head was painful in both his neck and his ribcage.

"We should get you to a doctor," the officer said, following Gus into his office and watching anxiously as he sank down slowly into his leather chair.

"What happened?" Jessica Martin, the lieutenant commander of the department, Gus' second in command, stalked into the office and looked at the chief with concern. "You look like crap."

"He was hit by a car this morning on his run," Purcival told her. "I think he needs medical attention."

"No shit," Jessica snapped. She reached over and picked up the phone on Gus' desk and punched in some numbers. "Yeah, this is Lt. Martin," she said. "Chief Haddock is injured and needs emergency care, stat. He's in his office. Send an EMT over here right away."

Gus groaned in his chair. "I don't need the medics," he said. "Just a couple of bruises. I'll live."

"Shut up, chief," Jessica said. She paused and looked at him. "Respectfully speaking, of course."

Gus smiled and just nodded.

Two minutes later, Billy Connors, one of the town's uniformed emergency responders rushed into the room, carrying his mobile kit and began pulling on a pair of blue nitrile gloves. He crouched down in front of Gus and reached up to examine his facial bruises first. "What hurts the most?" he asked.

"Ribs, probably," Gus managed to say. "Might be broken. Left knee, too."

"Right," the EMT said. He passed his hands quickly and surely over Gus, feeling for ragged edges in the ribcage and testing the flex of his left knee. "I think we need to take you in for X-rays," he said. "Get an orthopedist to take a look at that knee."

"I don't have time for …" Gus started to say. Jessica Martin cut him off.

"Don't play the big strong man, Gus," she said. "It's bull-shit and you know it. You've got some serious injuries and you need to take care of them, right now."

Gus sat back as if in surrender. "Can I at least get a cup of coffee?" he said.

Jessica smiled. "A to-go cup," she said, and nodded at the EMT. He turned to the mic on his shoulder and ordered the ambulance to pull around to the front of the police station.

It was midafternoon when Gus returned to the station. This time, his ribcage was wrapped in bandages and he had an aluminum crutch to help him keep his weight off his left knee. And he had been given some pain medication which helped with the pain for sure. It also made him feel a little loopy.

He limped into his office, plopped down in his leather desk chair and immediately felt a lot better. Surrounded by familiar things again. Even if those things were only his desk telephone, blotter and a growing stack of While You Were Out slips rep-resenting people who had called him since this morning. He looked at the stack and smiled to himself.

Jessica Martin and Buzz Franklin, the Little Penwick PD's chief of detectives, came into the office and sat in the chairs in front of the desk. Both looked at Gus, concerned.

"How you feelin' chief?" Buzz asked.

"Feelin' no pain," Gus said, smiling. "The wonders of chemistry."

Buzz nodded, then got serious. "We've been out to Indian Hill Road," he said. "Took a look around."

"Bet you didn't find anything," Gus said. "There's nothing on that road, except for three houses and one farm. That's why I run there most mornings."

"I talked to the homeowners," Buzz continued. "Nobody saw anything this morning. Mrs. Gilligan said she sees you running early all the time, but doesn't remember seeing you today. She said that local kids sometimes speed down that road — it's a long straightaway, mostly flat, so it's a good place to crank it up if you're trying to impress a girl or something."

"My friend Tom in high school had a Dodge Charger, 426 Hemi engine, fire engine red," Gus said. "Or at least his Dad did. But he would take me out for a spin and used to see if he could get it up to a hundred on Indian Hill. Kids are crazy. It's a miracle any of us survived to adulthood."

"Anyway, nobody seems to have seen anything this morning," Buzz continued. "Do you remember anything about the car? Make? Model? Color?"

Gus looked at Buzz, who seemed to be surrounded by a glowing aura. It was quite interesting, the way the aura sort of pulsed and glowed at the same time. Then he shook his head and tried to come back to reality.

"No," he said. "Happened too fast. By the time I picked myself up, it was gone."

"Do you think it was deliberate?" Jessica asked. "Were they trying to run you down?"

Gus shook his head. "Nah," he said. "Why would someone do that? I haven't done anything to anyone. Probably just someone fiddling with their radio or trying to text. Didn't see me until it was too late."

Jessica and Buzz looked at each other, eyebrows raised.

"I can think of one somebody who'd like to turn you into roadkill," Buzz said.

"Whozzat?" Gus said.

"Janine Stone," Buzz said. "Just for starters. Attorney General Preston Knox for another. And maybe even Ricky Giancarlo up at the Big Daddy Lounge. He's probably pretty pissed at you these days."

Gus waved a hand in dismissal. "Naw," he said. "Buncha crap."

"Chief," Jessica said, leaning over his desk. "I think you need to take the rest of the afternoon off. You're not in any condition to make any decisions right now. Go home and get some rest. See how you feel in the morning."

"I'm gonna call ICE," Buzz said. "They told you a couple weeks ago they had some reports that Janine had come back into the country down in Miami. We should find out what else they know."

"She's not coming back here," Gus said. "She knows we'll bust her soon as she steps foot in Little Penwick."

"Yeah, well let me find out what they know first," Buzz said, "Then we can determine what to do."

Gus looked at Buzz but suddenly couldn't quite focus on him. His head began to wobble and he finally let it flop back and rest against the back of his chair. He closed his eyes.

"Buzz," Jessica Martin said. "Take the chief home and make sure he's sleeping before you leave."

"Right," Buzz said.

The next morning, Gus awoke in his apartment above the two-car garage belonging to his landlady, Mrs. Vera Phillips. He looked at his phone and was amazed to see it was just past nine o'clock. He usually awoke around five. Then he swung his legs off the bed and tried to stand up.

"Ahhh," he said, out loud.

Everything in his body hurt. His knee was throbbing, his ribs were barking, the back of his left arm was sore to the touch and his head hurt. *Guess I'm not running today*, he thought.

He managed to get in the shower and stood there for ten minutes, first in scalding hot water, which made some of his hurt parts feel a little better. Then he turned the control to cold and stood in the freezing needles as long as he could stand it. When he finally climbed out, his skin was pink, but his body felt measurably better. He toweled off, shaved and managed to make himself coffee, which he drank standing up next to the counter.

Getting dressed was the next challenge, and Gus discovered that if he sat down on the bed, he could bend over and get the opening of his left pants leg over the top of his foot and pull it up slowly without yelling at the pain. The right leg went easier and the rest was fairly straightforward. Although stretching his hands above his head made his ribs bark a little louder. The doctor from the hospital had prescribed some more pain pills, and, reluctantly, Gus swallowed one before making his way slowly down the stairs and climbing into his squad car.

When he arrived at the station, it was ten-thirty and except for Freddie Benes at the front desk, there was no one in sight. Freddie greeted him, asked how he was feeling and told him that everyone was in the conference room at the back of the station. Gus nodded, went to the break room for another cup of coffee and continued down the hall.

When he opened the door to the conference room, he saw Jessica Martin at the head of the table, and next to her was Buzz Franklin. Two other chairs held two men Gus didn't recognize at first. The first man turned, as did everyone else, when Gus walked in, and Gus nodded at him in recognition.

"Dennis," he said, "How you been?"

"Better than you, it seems," the man named Dennis said with a grin and stood to shake Gus' hand. Dennis Frechette was the head of the Immigration and Customs Enforcement office in Providence, someone Gus had met back when he was a patrolman for the Little Penwick force. Even though Frechette was a fed, Gus liked him. He didn't know the other man.

"Gus, this is Agent Rick Winchester," Frechette said, indicating him. "He's on assignment to our office."

"Agent Winchester," Gus said, shaking his hand, "Welcome to Little Penwick."

"Thanks," Winchester said. "Dennis tells me you got some good seafood down here."

Gus looked at him with a small smile. "We do," he said. "You can get it either at one of our restaurants, or I can show you the mud flats below Round Pond. They say the quahogs there are as big as softballs. It's free to dig your own. They make for excellent stuffies."

"Not sure what a stuffie is," Agent Winchester said, "But I'm sure they're good."

"Stuffed clams, Rick," Frechette said. "Usually made with the meat of the larger clams known around here as quahogs. Kind of the specialty of the region down here." He looked at Gus. "He's originally from St. Louis," he said in explanation.

"Explains a lot," Gus said and motioned for both the agents to sit down. They did.

"If we're done with the social hour, let's get back to it," Jessica Martin said. "First, Chief, how are you feeling today?"

"Better," Gus lied. "Got about twelve hours of sleep last night and woke up feeling semi-human again. Thanks for making me go home."

Jessica nodded, satisfied.

"Buzz talked yesterday afternoon to Agent Frechette here," she said, nodding at those two. "He asked for an updated report on Janine Stone. Agent Frechette said he would rather come here today and brief us in person. He had just started when you got here, Chief."

Gus nodded. "Keep going," he said. "I'm listening."

Frechette took the floor. "We starting tracking Ms. Stone last Thanksgiving, after your officers let her slip away," he said, opening a file folder in front of him.

Gus held up a hand. "Let me just say that while she may have evaded arrest, in the middle of a big bust of a human trafficking ring, a bust developed and executed by the officers of this department, it was all you alphabet soup federal agencies that let her disappear into the ether," he said. "Just for the record."

Frechette nodded. "Duly noted," he said. "As I was saying, we started taking a serious look at her after that. She went onto everybody's radar. We picked up some indications that she was in Brazil for a while, down to Argentina, then Mexico City. There are a few gaps in the record, but it seems she has been mostly in South and Latin America since January."

"Doing what?" Gus asked.

"Not sure," Frechette said. "We never had eyes on her 24/7. And she's smart enough not to use the same cellphone or debit or credit card more than once. And those all turned out to be burners or pre-paid. But little blips came up here and there, so we could put together a reasonable facsimile of her movements over the last six months."

"You called me when you had word that she had returned into the country in Miami last month," Gus said. "Why didn't you pick her up?"

"We didn't know it was her until after the fact," Frechette said. "She came in under a false passport, different name, new appearance. But one of our facial recognition cameras ID'd her, after the fact." He paused and shook his head sadly. "We're trying to get the technology to work faster, simultaneous to the subject being in line, but with her new name and appearance, she was able to get through Customs before the ID system kicked her out for review. It was her, though. I've seen the photos. It's her."

"Where is she now?" Gus asked.

Frechette shrugged. "Don't know," he said. "But we're thinking she's coming back here."

"Why do you think that?" Buzz Franklin asked.

Frechette turned to his partner, who sat up a little straighter.

"Ms. Stone had been operating a very successful human smuggling operation here," Winchester said. "She was working for, and being paid quite well, by the local criminal elements who run the strip clubs and prostitution rings both here in Rhode Island and all over New England."

"That'd be Ricardo Giancarlo's operation," Gus said.

"Correct," Winchester said, nodding. "She was very good at recruiting and training. We think it's very likely she's coming back to set up her op again. She knows Giancarlo and his people will fund her. She just needs to figure out the players to help her set up a new operation. The local people here in Little Penwick she had are no longer available."

Gus nodded. "Danny Ferro and his uncle Cosmo are both doing five to ten in the federal joint up in Devens," he said. "The kid, Emilio, is at the ACI over in Cranston for the next two years."

"With miles of coastline and lots of hidden coves, rivers and backwaters, this part of the coast is perfect for smuggling," Winchester said. "Our estimation is that she'll look for another local patsy to help her move the women in and up to Providence."

Gus was frowning. "Why was she in South America for six months?" he said. "And Mexico?"

"Hiding out," Frechette said. "What else? Now she thinks things have cooled down, she's back and looking for action again."

"So what do you guys think we should do?" Gus asked. "Start setting up roadblocks? Door to door searches? Put her mug on every TV screen and newspaper front page. '*Have you seen this woman?*'"

Frechette shrugged. "That's entirely up to you, chief," he said. "It's your town. We're just sharing the information we have with our local law enforcement partner."

Gus looked at him for a moment or two. Then he nodded and stood up.

"OK, gentlemen," he said, "Thanks for coming down. And for sharing. We will take it from here."

Frechette stood up, then paused. "I can also tell you that we've approved satellite surveillance of this area," he said. "We've got eyes in the sky looking out for any unusual maritime activity."

Gus smiled. "Good luck on that," he said. "This time of year there are probably ten thousand pleasure boats out in Rhode Island Sound. If your satellites can tell me which ones are full of bad guys, I'd be impressed."

He turned to Winchester. "If you take Main Road back north, look for a little place called Evelyn's on Nanaquacket Pond," he said. "They've got the best stuffies around these parts. Its in the next town from ours, but they buy their quahogs from people around here."

"Thanks, chief," Winchester said, shaking his hand. "I think we will."

CHAPTER 3

AFTER THE ICE agents left, Gus told Jessica and Buzz to stay. His various aches and pains had dulled, no doubt thanks to the pain medication, and he was able to concentrate.

"How are you doing, Gus?" Jessica asked him, looking concerned. "Really? If you need to take more time to recover, we can hold down the fort." She was in her fifties, her blondish hair picking up a few strands of gray here and there. She wore the full uniform, including a dark tie, striped pants and black polished shoes. "Whoever it was that knocked you into the ditch came close. Too close."

Gus Haddock shrugged. "I've survived worse," he said. "Some Afghan guy jumped on me, hiding in the rafters in some barn we were clearing out near Awbeh, east of Herat. He stabbed my upper arm before Jocko took him out. A little bloody, but I was good to go once they wrapped me up."

"She didn't ask about old war stories, chief," Buzz Franklin said, "She wants to know how you're doing right now." Franklin was dressed in his usual disheveled street clothes, which looked like it had been weeks, if ever, since he had last used an iron. Buzz might look like he slept in his clothes, but he had an intuitive mind, never forgot an important fact and seemed to know everybody in law enforcement throughout Rhode Island and beyond.

Gus fixed his chief of detectives with an even stare. "I'm good," he said. "Slight fracture in two of my ribs, but there's nothing they can do about that until they heal. Knee is sprained. If I can keep the weight off of it for a few days, I should be right as rain." He paused and looked at the two of them. "Now let's talk about Janine and what we can do about her."

Buzz stared back for an instant or two, and then shrugged. *You don't want to talk about it? OK by me.*

"If the feds are right, she's back in town looking to set up shop again," Jessica said. "It would help if we could get a photo of her new look. Then we could brief the force to be on the lookout for her. I doubt if she'll still be tooling around town in her bright yellow Miata."

Gus nodded. "Buzz, call Frechette and ask him to send us that Customs photo he was looking at. Should be a good enough likeness."

"Right, chief," Buzz said.

Gus paused, thinking. "The first thing you said … *if the feds are right* … seems important to me. Because I'm thinking they are not right about this."

"You don't think she's back in town?" Buzz said. "Or coming back to town?"

Gus shook his head. "No, I think she *is* here, or will be," he said. "But I don't think she's coming back to start up her operation again."

"Why not, chief?" Jessica asked, cocking her head to one side.

"Janine Stone is a loner," Gus said. "She set up her entire operation last time by herself. The goombahs in Providence gave her funds and lots of freedom to do what she wanted to do. But she drove that operation. She recruited the women. She planned how to get them in and how to move them around New England. She was lucky to find Danny Ferro, who is something of a mechanical genius. We don't know who came up with the idea to re-purpose an oil truck and turn it into a people mover, but that was brilliant."

"But even if the whole smuggling thing was Janine's idea and she made it work, why wouldn't she want to crank it up again?" Jessica pressed.

"Too predictable," Gus said. "Janine is a chess player. She knows that doing the same move again is too obvious. You've got to mix up your moves, your strategy, or you get killed. In chess, at least."

"The ICE guys seem to think she's coming back to do it again," Buzz said,

"You know that saying, that generals are always fighting the last war?" Gus said, looking at Buzz, "I can tell you from experience that the Intelligence guys and probably the ICE guys are guilty of the same thing. If X did Y once, they think X will do Y over and over again, forever. It always surprises them when X instead does Z, or even A and B."

"And you think she's coming back to do something entirely different?" Jessica said. "Like what?"

"I don't know," Gus said, frowning. "I haven't figured that part out yet."

The door to the conference room opened and Dottie Adams, the department's indefatigable dispatcher, walked in with a box of donuts. "These just got delivered by a secret admirer," Dottie said, smiling at everyone around the table. "I thought you guys might need a sugar high. Seems like you're pondering big things in here."

She passed the box to Gus, who took out a jelly donut and smiled his thanks at Dottie.

"You feeling OK chief?" she asked him, concern in her voice. "We heard that you got run over yesterday."

"They missed me, Dottie," Gus said with a smile. He held up a hand with his first two fingers pressed together. "Missed me by *that* much."

"The gossip in the station is that awful Janine Stone did it," Dottie continued around the table, passing out the donuts. Jessica smiled and shook her head in refusal. Buzz Franklin took two.

"Maybe," Jessica told her. "We're trying to figure out why she would come back to Little Penwick."

"Duh," Dottie said, as if the answer was obvious. "Remember what Chief Julius always used to say? 'Follow the money.' She's come back because someone owes her money. Or didn't pay her the last time."

With a wave of her hand, Dottie left the conference room. The three police officers looked at each other for a moment or two, then broke out in shared laughter.

"Out of the mouths of babes," Buzz chortled. "Not that I think our Dottie is a babe."

That made Jessica howl even more.

When they all calmed down, Gus was nodding. "She's right, you know," he said. "It's always about the money." He turned to Buzz. "Did anyone ever discuss finances during the trials a few months ago?"

Buzz shook his head. "Nope," he said. "We know payments were made. The Giancarlo group was paying Janine a flat fee, amount unknown. She used that fee to cover expenses, like paying Danny Ferro to buy the old oil truck and turn it into a passenger bus without windows. That must have taken a wad of cash."

"She did leave town in a hurry," Gus said, remembering that cold night at the Little Penwick harbor when he and his officers intercepted the arrival of a new group of smuggled women and arrested Danny Ferro and his uncle Cosmo on the docks. But in the confusion and hubbub, Janine Stone was able to escape on a fast powerboat she had purposefully had ready for just such an emergency. The boat was later found, abandoned, on Long Island. She disappeared and, from what ICE said, fetched up in South America.

"OK, Buzz, let's start a new assumption," Gus said. "That Janine Stone left behind an unknown sum of money from her smuggling operation, and has come back to collect it."

"That works," Buzz nodded. "If it's a significant amount, that would justify her coming back to collect it. Then she could go somewhere else and start a new smuggling operation. or something else. Somewhere where she's not as well known. Where she can start fresh."

Gus nodded. "I like that. Now ... where would that money be?"

"I'll check with all the local banks," Buzz said. "See if any of them have accounts in the name of Janine Stone. Or if any have made any unusual cash disbursements in the last few weeks."

"Janine Stone doesn't strike me as the kind that would leave her money in a bank account," Jessica said. "Too easy to be traced, discovered, frozen. She'd want her funds in ready cash. And if she did have an account, for some reason, she could just order a transfer to a new account, anywhere in the world. No reason to come back to town to get it."

"So it's hidden," Gus said. "Where?"

Jessica and Buzz looked at each other. Then they spoke in unison.

"The Ferro's" they said.

Gus nodded again. "Yeah, that makes sense," he said. "That family has been involved in all kinds of crazy schemes and illegal activities for a couple generations now. And their land is full of old ponds and swamps and empty wood lots. Plenty of places to hide some cash."

"Can we get a warrant and go search?" Jessica said.

Gus was shaking his head. "I doubt it," he said. "We need a specific location before a judge will approve a search warrant. I don't think we can get away with saying we suspect the Ferros have buried a load of cash somewhere on their 200 acres. We've got to narrow it down, somehow."

Buzz sat up straight as an idea came to him. "What about ICE's eye in the sky?" he said. "I can ask Frechette to concentrate the satellite surveillance to the Ferro property. If they see a guy going out into the woods with a shovel, we can move in."

Gus chuckled. "Good idea, but I'm not sure that will work," he said. "But when you talk to Frechette about Janine's new picture, ask them if they can get that specific."

"Right," Buzz nodded.

Gus stood up, a little unsteadily, and stood there, waiting for the muscles in his legs and trunk to stop hurting and start moving.

"OK guys," he said. "I've got dinner plans. Let's reconvene again Monday morning."

"Hot date?" Buzz asked with a smirk.

"Maggie's down for the weekend," Gus said. He began walking back toward his office. Or limping, since he needed his aluminum crutch.

"Hope you weren't planning on getting lucky," Buzz said. "Doesn't look like that's gonna work."

Gus leveled a glare. "That part's not busted," he said, a bit grimly.

Jessica Martin made a disapproving sound. Buzz laughed and patted Gus on the back.

"Go get 'em, tiger," he said.

CHAPTER 4

I ALMOST HAD *him. He was right in my sights. Don't know how I missed him.*

Oh, I suppose I really didn't want to hurt old Gus. He's not bad looking, for a cop. It was pure serendipity that I passed by him that morning when he was running. I can't remember why I was driving down that road at that time of morning. I was on my way over to New Bedford to meet a guy. Then I saw this man running and as I passed him, I saw it was Gus Haddock, the chief of police.

Something made me turn around and come back down that road the other way. I was behind him now. It would have been easy as pie to nail him from behind. To just run right over him, hear the thump-thump of the wheels running over his body. Maybe hear him scream a little. Of course, that would have left a mark on my car and that would have attracted attention from somebody. A bloody dent in your front quarter usually is a dead giveaway. Hah! I made a pun.

I'm trying to lay low. It's pretty easy to blend in, even in a small town like Little Penwick. My hair is black now. I like it better than the mousy brown I first used when I left town.

Black is the color of power. Strength. You don't mess around with a woman with jet black hair. You stay out of her way.

I like feeling powerful. I felt that way for a couple years, after I first came up here to work in Ricardo's clubs. Those pathetic bastards who slip you bills and think that means they own you, even for a few minutes for a lap dance or more … they don't realize that all the power is with me. I can smile and flirt and show them a little this or that, and they're like putty in my hands. Their eyes go out of focus and they lick their lips like they've been crawling across the desert or something and would do anything for a sip of water. I control them. And if they get rough or rude or out of hand, all I have to do is look at one of the bouncers and boom! End of problem.

I spent about six months doing that and then I went to see Ricardo and told him how I could help his business. I spelled it out for him. I was just talking, but now I know that I could have done one of those Powerpoint things, like they teach in the business school. I didn't need that. My ideas were good. I knew it would work. I knew I could do it.

After we got busted, they sent me down here to Little Penwick to live with Margie Almeida, one of the Ferro family. Margie was like a second mother to me, took me under her wing. Told me what was going on and who the players were. She helped me refine my plan, helped get me a meet with Ricardo. Margie always told me not to take crap from anyone, but especially not from a man. She taught me how to use what I have, how to use it to good effect, to get what I want. I cried for a week when Margie passed. She was the mother and grandmother I never had, even though I had both in real life.

Still do, actually, although I never see them anymore. That's another story.

And Danny, of course. I lived in his house. His wife Catarina didn't like that, not one bit, but Danny sure did. Man, oh man, did he have a case for me! I mean, always with the big hopeful eyes, jumping to get me anything I wanted, pasted on smiling face all the time. Talk about pussy-whipped ... Danny would have jumped off the Empire State building if I asked him to. So I asked him to come up with some new way to transport a dozen or so women so nobody would stop us and he did. That oil truck with the hydraulic lift in the back was a thing of beauty. Amazing!

I figured out how men can be affected by their secret desires a long, long time ago. My father began abusing me when I was eleven. 'Abusing.' What a pansy word that is. What he did was, he came into my bathroom when I was having my bath and insisted on soaping my back. I didn't want him to, I was at that age when my privacy was super important. But he insisted and then he did and it wasn't just my back that he wanted to soap. And touch.

Mother dearest was useless. She's out to lunch most of the time. Had no idea what her beloved husband was doing. No idea. Wondering why I was acting out in school a lot, and with my friends, getting into all kinds of trouble. I was screaming for help, for someone to come along and stop it. But nobody did.

But I learned some things. When a man is so into that kind of thing, you can get him to do anything. Which is how I got the latest gamer stuff. And an I-phone, newest model. A new bike. Oh my God, the clothes and shoes! I'd say it was magnificent, but not for what I had to do to get all that stuff. That wasn't magnificent. It was sick.

Anyway, Danny and I worked well together. He did what I told him to do. We worked and refined and improved the plan and then it started working. Better and better. I was bringing in some quality inventory and Ricardo and his people were putting them to work and everyone was making scads of money.

Money. I didn't care about it all that much, tell you the truth. I just liked making my plan work. I used some of my money to buy a car, a Miata. Loved that car. Put the top down in the summer and it was like flying. As for the rest ... Margie made dinner every night. Danny asked me to stay in his house, Catarina to the contrary. So what did I need money for? OK, that was a little naive on my part, I admit.

Danny said he'd take care of it. He collected the cash from Ricardo and brought it down to Little Penwick and used it to cover his expenses. I was never even sure how much they were giving him. I didn't care. I was young and stupid. Now I'm not. Well, not stupid anymore, that I can tell you.

So now, Danny is in jail. Margie is dead. Catarina refuses to see me or talk to me. Nobody wants to talk about my money. Where it is. How much it is. How I can get it.

But I will. Get it. And then I'm out of this place for good. Met some interesting people down in Buenos Aires and they said they'd love to have me come down and work with them. I need an ante, though. An upfront indication of my seriousness. I get that. So I need my money.

I need it now. And I'm going to get it. That's the most important thing.

But seeing Gus Haddock lying dead in a ditch would have been great! A bonus!

But I guess I flinched, right at the last second. I'll have to think about that. Figure out why I did that. So that next time, I won't do it again.

CHAPTER 5

With Maggie down for the weekend, Gus bought some rib eyes to grill. Mrs. P had a fancy propane grill on her deck with lots of bells and whistles, and Gus always used it. In exchange, he invited Mrs. P to join them for the meal. Maggie and Mrs. P had become good friends during the months when she had been the Special Master for the Little Penwick PD, and after, and the two women added to the evening's menu with some baked potatoes and a pan of sliced and chopped vegetables, tossed in olive oil, that Gus sauteed on one of the side burners of Mrs. P's fancy grill.

Gus had opened a bottle of wine and poured three glasses, and they were sitting on Mrs. P's back deck, enjoying the smells of roasting meat and the quiet of the back yard and the thick woods beyond. The day was warm and the setting sun made dappled patterns on the green lawn. Birds flitted back and forth, chasing the last of their insect meals before the sun set.

Both women had made a big deal out of Gus' injuries from his close encounter with an automobile. They tried to make him sit and let them handle all the food preparation, but he insisted on overseeing at least the grilling of the meat. He had downed another pain pill when he got back from the station, and that helped with both his physical aches, and his general attitude toward the world. He sipped on his wine, but went slowly with that, understanding that there might be some side effects mixing alcohol with his pain meds.

Maggie brought Gus and Mrs. P up to date with news of her new non-profit to help abused women. She'd been successful in getting a nice grant from the Rhode Island Foundation, probably the state's largest supporter of good causes, which had enabled her to add one paid staffer and a couple of part timers to help.

"It's been a Godsend," she said, pushing her curly hair back from her forehead. "For the first time in a year, I've had a little time to think and plan. Shaki helps with the day-to-day counseling and processing, the part timers answer the phone and call suppliers when we need something. And I get to think about what we do next."

"And what is that, dear?" Mrs. P asked. Gus flipped the steaks over. They were nice and brown, slightly charred.

"Once we get the women out of their abusive situations, we work with them and try to find a safe place for them to live and then to try and arrange employment," she said. "I've started working with various shelter organizations in Providence and elsewhere in the state, looking for beds. Then we try to find them a place to work, so they can start to earn money and get their feet back under them."

She sighed. "It's a long process, and it's never one that goes in a straight line," she said. "Believe it or not, we've had several clients who go back to their old places, back to the abuse. I'll never understand why, but some go back."

"The devil you know is better, sometimes, than the one you don't," Gus said. "They may appreciate all you are doing for them, but they can't imagine standing on their own two feet. They feel more comfortable back in the space where they were. Even if it means getting whacked around sometimes."

"Or worse," Maggie said. "We had a client who was murdered a month ago. She went back with her boyfriend. He killed her a week later." She fingered her glass of wine. "I still haven't gotten over that one."

"And hopefully, you never will, dear," Mrs. P said. "That is just unimaginably horrible."

Maggie shook her head as if to clear away the darkness.

"So, Mister Policeman," she said, "Have you discovered which deviant resident of Little Penwick tried to run you over the other day?"

"Not yet," Gus admitted as he turned the steaks over again. He prodded at them with his tongs and decided another three or four minutes would get them right into that medium-rare sweet spot. "Nobody saw the actual car, including me, so it's a little hard to chase after a ghost. But we're thinking about someone we suspect might be involved."

"Who's that, dear?" Mrs. P asked.

"Our old friend, the lovely Janine Stone," Gus said, flipping the steaks one more time. The juices spilled onto the hot fake coals and hissed, sending up a cloud of fragrant steam.

"I thought she left the country," Maggie said, taken aback. "You mean she's back in Little Penwick?"

Gus smiled at her. "She might be," he said. "There have been no official sightings yet, so it's all just conjecture. But she might be here. And if she is, she'd have reason to run me over!"

"I hope you've ordered extra security," Maggie said. She looked upset at this news. "That woman is a menace to society."

"Oh, I think we can handle it," Gus said, poking one more time at the steaks. "We've got a new photo of her. She's got dark hair now. Everyone on the force has a copy and they're all on the lookout. If she sticks her head up, we'll be there to grab her."

He picked up the smallest steak, the one most done, and turned to transfer it to the serving platter next to the grill. The movement made him groan a little as his ribs protested.

"See?" Maggie was watching him carefully. "You're in no condition to catch a fly right now. Gus, I'm worried. I think you should call in the state police. Have them send a squad down. You can't be too careful with someone like her."

"We don't need the staties," Gus said, moving the other two steaks over to the platter. He kept his molars tightly locked to prevent any further sounds from emanating from his mouth while he did so. "I'm going to be mostly sitting at my desk for the next week, letting the bod heal and letting my officers look for the woman. Maybe I can't run after her right now, but I can out-think her." He turned and looked at them. "Let's eat," he said.

The two women went inside and came back out with a bowl of salad, plates, silverware, place mats and napkins. They set the table while Gus carried the serving platter to the table and put the veggie pan on a hot pad. He turned off the gas, sat down and they passed around the food and began to eat. Gus refilled his glass of wine, and topped up Mrs. P's. He noticed that Maggie's wine had gone mostly untouched. Mrs. P's Irish setter, which had been exploring the back yard, smelled the meat and came and sat down at her feet, his limpid eyes staring up at her hopefully. She smiled and slipped him a little slice of steak. He swallowed it whole and looked up with his expressive eyes, as if to ask *Please sir, may I have some more?*

To change the subject, Gus began talking about the search for two new patrol officers to replace the two who were leaving at the end of the summer. He told them he had received a couple dozen resumes and was slowly sifting through them.

"You're going to hire a woman, right?" Maggie said. "Hopefully, a woman of color. Has Little Penwick ever had a woman officer?"

"I think Jess Martin, my second in command, is a woman," Gus said, chewing happily on his steak. "At least she was, last time I looked."

"You know what I mean," Maggie said. "I mean starting out from scratch. Are there any women in your list of candidates?"

Gus nodded. "Yeah, a couple," he said.

"Well, there you go," Maggie said. "Hire 'em both. Set a new standard. Make a statement."

"More wine?" Gus said, picking up the bottle and holding it out. Maggie shook her head, declining.

"My job is to find the best possible candidate who would be successful as a police officer in a small town like ours," Gus said. "I am not averse to hiring a woman, or a black person, or any other color or flavor you got. But the important thing is to find someone who will fit in, be successful in this kind of environment. That means I need to interview them, get to know them, make a judgment as to their fitness. It's more complicated that just the color of their skin or the variety of what's inside their skivvies."

Mrs. P laughed at that, which made her start choking a little. Gus stood up in case a Heimlich was required, but Mrs. P held up a hand. "I'm OK," she said. "Don't make me laugh when I'm eating. Went down the wrong way."

She daubed at her watering eyes with her napkin. "As a citizen of this town, I approve of your hiring strategy," she said. "As a woman, I agree wholeheartedly with Maggie here. This town could use a little shake-up in the ranks. I hope you can find a good female candidate. Or two."

The sun slipped below the horizon and the twilight deepened. Gus filled up a tray with the dishes from the meal and was going to carry them inside. Maggie and Mrs. P told him to sit down, they'd take care of it. They went into the kitchen and began making coffee, chattering about this and that while they did. Gus could hear them tittering as they worked in the kitchen.

Gus sat by himself on the back deck, his injured leg elevated on an ottoman. The setter curled up around his other foot and went to sleep with a heavy dog sigh. It was quiet and peaceful. Most of the birds had departed for their nests and roosts and even the insects, singing in their rhythmic buzzing in the nearby swamps, seemed to reach a lower, slower key.

Suddenly, Gus caught a flash of something grey and white blasting across the back yard before swooping upwards into the top of a nearby pine.

The women came out with coffee and cookies.

"I just saw a barn owl fly across the yard," Gus reported. "He's gone up there." He pointed at the tree.

"Oh, yes," Mrs. P said. "I see him from time to time. Usually around this time of day. I think they like to hunt at night."

"I wonder what an owl sighting means, symbolically?" Maggie said.

Gus said "Good luck" at the exact time that Maggie said "Bad luck" and they both laughed. Mrs. P poured them each a cup of coffee and Gus ate one of the cookies.

"God, I really love the peace and quiet down here," Maggie said as she sipped at her coffee. "Up in Providence, in my apartment, I hear sirens going by, and cars honking and it's just noise all the time. You actually get used to it and manage to ignore it. But then you come down here, and it's totally amazing and peaceful not to hear anything at all."

A few minutes later, both Maggie and Mrs. P yawned at the same moment. "Even a mouth-breathing, knuckle-dragging person of the male persuasion can tell it's time to say goodnight," Gus said. "Can I help with the dishes?"

"Already done, young man," Mrs. P said. "You and your lovely young friend are excused, with my thanks for a lovely meal on a lovely evening."

They bid her good night and walked across the driveway and up the stairs to Gus' apartment. Maggie helped Gus limp up the stairs, his left leg held straight, knee unflexed. He unlocked the door and they went inside.

Maggie went to use the bathroom first. Gus sank down into his couch, propped his leg up and turned on the television to get a score of the Red Sox game. He kept the sound on mute, because the quiet of the evening was nicer than blaring announcers or, worse, noisome ads for tire stores, beer brands and furniture stores.

In a few minutes, Maggie came into the living room, wearing a terrycloth robe she had left behind and wiping the last of some cream off her face.

"Who's winning?" she asked, fluffing out her hair with her fingers.

"Sox by three," Gus said. "Barkin has been throwing the ball like a champ the last few outings."

Maggie sat down next to Gus on the couch and, pulling a little metal tool of some kind out of a pocket of her robe, began doing something to her nails and cuticles.

"I noticed you didn't touch the wine tonight," he said after a bit. "Not feeling well? Or don't you like cabernet sauvignon?"

She continued fussing with her nails. He waited. She fussed with another. Then she put the tool down and began to cry.

"It's OK," Gus said softly, reaching over and grabbing her hand. "If you didn't like the wine, I don't mind. It's perfectly OK to ..."

"I'm pregnant, you idiot," she said, shoulders shaking. "I'm going to have your baby."

There was a deep silence in the room that lasted several minutes. Gus stared at the silent television. A Red Sox batter knocked a ball off the Green Monster and trotted easily into second. The batter clapped his hands together, then waved at his teammates in the dugout. Gus barely paid attention. His mind was racing a million miles an hour.

"That's great," Gus said, finally.

"I'm so sorry," Maggie said almost at the same instant. "I never meant this to happen. I mean, not yet." She began weeping even harder. "I mean, what the hell are we going to do?"

Gus reached over and pulled Maggie into his embrace, his arms reaching around and pulling her against his chest. She let go then, and began to shake as she let her emotions flow. He held her, rubbing her back and murmuring to her that it would be OK. They'd figure it out. After a time, her shaking and weeping subsided and she began to breath in regular tempo. He glanced down at her face and saw that she was asleep. Her face was reddened, her cheeks crossed with rivulets of her tears. She had thrown her arms around him, and she lay halfway across his body. He let her sleep. He had a million questions, and a million more things to say, but decided he could ask them later. Perhaps in the bright light of morning, when everything would look different.

So he let her sleep while he watched the end of the game in the silence of the dark apartment. He was excited by the news, of course, but also troubled. Their relationship was just six months old, more or less. He thought the world of Maggie. She was the one he wanted to tell about any news in his world. And he loved hearing her describe of the progress she was making in her new company. But they had not talked about taking it to the next level, whatever that might be. Live together? That would be hard to do, with him in Little Penwick and her in Providence. One of them would have to commute a pretty good distance. Were they in love? It felt like it, Gus thought. But what does love feel like? If you have to ask, do you really have it? He shook his head. *Too many questions. Not enough answers.* He remembered one of his commanders from Iran, Fallujah, who once said "Flying blind is no way to fight a war, or go through life. You gotta know exactly where you are and know exactly where you want to go. Then, and only then, can you decide the best way to get there."

Gus thought about that for a while. The ball game ended—the Sox won—and the studio guys began the endless analyzing of the game. Silently, since the mute button was still in operation.

Don't know where we're going in the future Gus thought, *But right now, I'm in the living room and I'm heading for the bedroom.*

Gus managed to slide out from Maggie's embrace. He stood up, picked her up effortlessly in his arms and carried her into the bedroom. His ribs hurt when he picked her up, and he had to walk very carefully with his sore knee so he wouldn't drop her on her head. Somehow he managed and laid her down on the bed. She slept through the whole thing.

CHAPTER
6

IN THE MORNING, Gus was drinking coffee and catching up on the news on his phone when Maggie came out of the bedroom, rubbing sleep from her eyes. Her hair was frizzed in wild patterns and she wore a big tee-shirt that came down to the top of her thighs.

"You're up early," she said, bending down to give him a kiss.

"I'm up early every day," Gus said. "I usually go running. But I'm still on injured reserve." He gestured at his knee. And paused. "And I couldn't sleep."

Maggie looked at him, then went and poured herself a cup of coffee in the kitchen. She came back and sat down next to him on the couch.

"OK," she said, after taking a fortifying sip. "Let's have it."

Gus started to say something, but Maggie held up a hand in a stop sign.

"No," she said. "Talk to me. You're upset. I understand. It's a big freakin' deal. Let's talk about it."

"Okay," Gus nodded. "How did this happen?"

She smiled. "Well, let's see," she said. "One, we take all our clothes off. Two, we do it. Three, your little swimmers do the backstroke up into my uterus. Four …"

"Okay, okay … stop," Gus said, trying to keep from snapping at her. They were walking on a knife's edge here, and he was trying to be empathetic, adult, intelligent and wise. "I know how it works. But we usually don't get pregnant. So how did *that* happen?"

She studied his face over the rim of her cup. Her eyes narrowed. "I am sensing some resentment," she said. "Along with a rather large dose of 'How did *you* let this happen.' Which is totally unfair of you. I mean, it does take two to tango, you know. Those little swimmers of yours didn't suddenly appear out of thin air."

Gus stood up and walked over to the window that looked down the driveway. It was another beautiful June morning, warm but not too hot, humidity at a comfortably dry level. But Gus wasn't thinking about the weather.

"I'm not blaming you, Maggie," he said. "Really, I'm not. Life is full of twists and turns, things that happen that you don't expect. I get all that. They told us in the Army that the best plan for battle lasts only until the first shots are fired. But this is a big one. I'm trying to get my head around it all."

"What part is the worst bit?" she asked. "That I unexpectedly got pregnant? Or that my being pregnant means you have to decide if you and I are a thing? Maybe you're not ready for this. I get that…"

"Is anyone ever ready for this?" Gus said.

She looked at him, a bit sadly. "Yes," she said. "Many people in a committed relationship decide to take the next step.

They live together. They often go through some kind of ceremony and invite friends and family to help them celebrate the new partnership. Then they decide to procreate, because they believe in their hearts that what they have is so good that it demands building a life and a family together."

"Yeah," Gus said, "That's probably the bit that I'm having the most trouble with. Usually, people in a committed relationship talk about where they are and where they want to go. They usually do that before they invite the parents to the wedding, and way before they decide to bring little juniors in the world."

"Ah," Maggie said. "So you're not ready."

"I didn't say that," Gus snapped. He couldn't help himself. "All I said was that people make these big decisions together. Usually after some times goes by. When they both know it's the right thing to do. It usually doesn't happen by accident."

"Well, it happened," she said.

"I know," he said.

She sipped some more coffee. Her heart was pumping at about eighty miles an hour. She felt like the rest of her life depended on what they said next.

"So you … no … so *we* gotta deal with it," she said finally.

"I know that," Gus said. "I'm trying to get there."

"Look," she said, "There are plenty of options here. You can decide you don't want to be in a relationship with me. Or that you don't want to be the father to this baby. That would be truly awful and would make me very sad. But I'd live. I can deal. This thing inside me is nothing but a clump of clotted blood and some snot. At least right now. I could …"

She had to stop talking. Her throat had constricted to the size of a human hair. Her eyes watered, but she willed herself not to cry.

"I don't want you to do that," he said softly. "That's not what I want."

"That's not what I want, either," she said.

They sat quietly for a moment or two.

"Look," she said finally. "Take the baby part away for a minute. Pretend that didn't happen. OK? So, I'm pretty sure I love you with all my heart."

"*Pretty* sure?" he said with a wry smile, his eyes glancing at her.

"*Very* sure," she said. "My heart tells me that you are a good man, with strong values. A decent man who wants to help others. A man who would do whatever it takes to support me and make me happy. And my heart tells me that I want to do the same for you."

"I love you, too," he said. "And I want to be with you."

"Okay!" she said in a gush. She felt relieved. Her heart rate calmed down. "That's a good start, right?"

He nodded.

"Now, we haven't known each other all that long," she continued. "And we really haven't talked … at all … about where our relationship might go someday."

"No, we haven't," he said.

"But despite that, I think we've both been thinking the same thing," she said. "I think we're on the same page. I think of us as a couple. Do you?"

"Yes," he said.

"In every way."

"Yes."

"Which means that, even if we haven't discussed it out loud, using words, we both are thinking that some day, when the time is right and the stars are aligned, we will take the next steps together. Right?"

"I think so, yes," he said.

"So, since we agree on all that," she said. "We can see that what has happened is nothing but a blip. We've short-circuited the process. We've cut out the 'time is right' part and the waiting for the stars to line up part. Through no fault of our own, or, rather, because we screwed up, we've time-traveled through all that stuff and we're now at the cusp of stepping out on that yellow brick road. We don't know where it will lead us, we don't know what adventures, good or bad, may happen. But we're pretty much agreed to start that journey and see where it takes us. Together."

Gus looked at her. Her eyes were bright. Her face a little flushed. She was holding on to her coffee cup like it was the only thing that could save her. Her knuckles were white with the effort.

"I guess that's right," Gus said. "But I gotta tell you, I always thought the Scarecrow was kinda creepy."

She smiled at him. "I'll keep the Scarecrow away," she said. "You work on the Wicked Witch."

He thought about that. Then he nodded.

"Deal," he said.

"Good," she said. "See? We've made some progress here. Despite what happened, or because of what happened, we agree that we're just beginning a new journey and it starts now."

"Yes," he said.

"And there might be some lingering feelings about the whole thing," she said, "Even some resentment. But as long as we are together, as a couple, we should be able to work those feelings out somehow."

Gus nodded. "Somehow," he said. "I might pout a little."

"A little is okay," she said. "More than a little? You need to talk to me."

"Okay," he said. "Where do we go from here? Where are we going to live? I don't think this place is good for raising babies." He looked around at the small apartment. "And I'm not sure I want to live in Providence and commute to work every day."

"Yes," Maggie said. "We need to talk about that."

"And what are we going to call it? And where is it going to school? And do we need a nanny?"

Maggie chuckled. "You have a lot of questions," she said.

"I'm just trying to figure out what comes next," he said.

"I have an idea," she said. "Why don't you take me back to bed and make sweet, sweet love to me," she said, reaching out with one hand to grab onto one of his. "I think that would be an excellent place to start."

"Can we do that?" he asked. "It won't hurt little Gus?"

She let go of his hand and smacked his shoulder, playfully. "You idiot," she said. "I'll let you know when we can't do that anymore." She leaned over and kissed him softly on the lips. "And just for the record, no child of mine will ever be named

'Gus'"

He nodded and stood up. "Okay," he said. "Nero is still open. Claudius, too. Lavinia if it's a girl."

He reached down and pulled her up into a standing position and they embraced. It lasted a long time. Both of their minds were still racing. But they had reached a new place. It still felt strange and ill-fitting, at least to Gus. But he felt less angst than he had when he awoke at five a.m.

"You may have to get on top," he said. "Don't think the knee is ready for that yet."

She pulled back and looked at him.

"The sacrifices we have to make," she said.

CHAPTER 7

BRIGHT AND EARLY Monday morning, Gus was standing in the bow of an enlarged inflatable Zodiac motor vessel as it skimmed at high speed across the water of the Sakonnet River, heading south toward Little Penwick. The sun was warm on his face, and the wind felt rejuvenating as it rushed past. He was feeling markedly better today, the aches and pains having subsided over the weekend. His left knee was still a little sore, but he could walk on it without wincing. Earlier that morning, getting ready for the day, he hadn't even had to down one of the last of his pain pills.

The boat belonged to the Law Enforcement Division of the state's Department of Environmental Management. Gus had driven up to a marina in Portsmouth, just north of the Old Stone Bridge and rendezvoused with Jack Benson, one of the DEM's Marine Enforcement officers. Benson was assigned to the Marine East watch, which covered the eastern half of Narragansett Bay, the Sakonnet River all the way from the state line in Mount Hope Bay down to the ocean, and along the coast. The DEM patrolled boaters, along with the Coast Guard, but was especially focused on enforcing fishing regulations. Saltwater anglers loved to catch striped bass—they were good fighters and delicious to eat—but the species had shown increasing scarcity in New England waters, which led to federal restrictions of no more than two fish a day, no less than 23 inches in length. So in addition to keeping an eye on the hundreds of small boats of fishermen, Benson was also charged with patrolling the waterfowl nesting areas, the shellfish banks, a growing number of oyster farms and anything else involving natural resources and the people who used and abused them.

Gus had asked Benson if he could ride with him on a patrol, to get a better idea of the coastal areas in and around Little Penwick, and they had agreed a few weeks ago to make this run. Standing in the bow, with the warm sun and the wind in his face, Gus felt himself begin to relax after what had turned out to be an emotional roller coaster of a weekend.

After their come-to-Jesus discussion on Saturday morning, Gus and Maggie had gone through the motions of enjoying a regular weekend. They made love. They went to the beach for a short walk—about all Gus' gimpy knee could stand. They went out for dinner at the Roadhouse and stayed to listen to the live band. They stumbled home late, each a little tipsy, and made love again. They slept late on Sunday and Gus brought out some of Alma's blueberry muffins for their Sunday breakfast.

But despite all that, something had changed, something was different. They both felt it. Some kind of invisible pall had fallen and they both knew it was there, between them. After coffee and muffins on Sunday, Maggie said she needed to get back to the city to work on a grant proposal that was due the following week. Gus walked her to her car and they embraced and kissed and she drove off. And Gus felt a little wave of relief. So he went into the station and pushed papers around for a few hours to punish himself.

Now, standing in the DEM boat as it sped down the river, watching the banks alternate between thin sandy beaches and rocky outcroppings, Gus felt the same way he had felt after a combat mission in the wilds of Afghanistan: slightly unbalanced, ears ringing, glad to be out of it, wondering what would happen next time.

Gus felt the boat slow as Benson steered it towards the eastern shore. He turned and went inside the small cabin in the center of the boat, where Jack was peering forward out of the windscreen. There was an array of electronic equipment and colorful radar screens on the dash in the helm station, and the radio, set to the nautical Channel 16, erupted from time to time with the fuzzy transmissions from the Coast Guard as well as from captains of other pleasure boats making their way around the waters of southern Rhode Island.

"Beautiful morning, isn't it?" Gus said to Jack when he came inside the cabin. Benson nodded, peering out as the boat neared the bank of the river. He was a short, stocky man in his forties. His skin was deeply tanned and he wore the DEM uniform of dark green chinos and shirt. "What are we doing?"

"I need to take some water samples over here," Benson said, pointing toward the shore. "There's a creek that drains into the river behind those rocks. The mud banks here are popular with the clammers. So I have to check for bacteria levels, bio-toxins and harmful algae blooms. We test on a weekly basis, but we like to test again after a few days of rain, because that's when a lot of the bad stuff gets washed into drains, flows into the river and affects the clams."

He guided the boat around some rocks and took her in close to the shore. The Zodiac didn't have much of a draft below the waterline—the twin propellers on the outboards were deeper than the keel. Gus could see the narrow creek with its dark brown water zig-zagging across a grassy tidal flat before disappearing into a stand of wind-stunted trees. Benson cut the boat's engines. He went outside and opened a cabinet on the back cockpit and took out a plastic tube weighted on one end, with a yellow nylon rope attached to the other. He went up to the bow, leaned over and dropped the contraption into the water, letting the yellow rope play out for a few feet. When he felt the weights hit the bottom, he pulled it up again. When the tube came out of the water, it was full. Benson carried the tube back to the cockpit and quickly filled several small containers with samples of the water. He capped and labeled them, stored them away in a plastic box and shut the cabinet door.

"I'll take samples today from about five or six more places," he told Gus. "Tonight, the lab rats up in Providence will do an analysis of the samples to see how much yucky stuff is in the water."

"Yucky stuff," Gus echoed. "That an official scientific term?"

Benson smiled, but said nothing, He cranked up the twin outboards and swung the boat's bow away from the shore and they headed back out into the river. He pointed to a part of the shoreline just south of the area where the creek and the mudflats were.

"Couple of farmers from Little Penwick have submitted a proposal to the state for permits to operate an oyster farm over there," he said. "The state is fine with the idea. All of Narragansett Bay and this part of the Sakonnet used to be wall-to-wall with natural oyster beds. Those little critters are not only delicious but they filter out a lot of the bad crap from the water. But in the early years of the twentieth century we over-harvested most of them and the rest croaked when the water in the Bay turned toxic, thanks to all the garbage we used to discharge into the Bay. Ever since we stopped dumping raw sewage and other stuff, the water quality has dramatically improved, so we hope the oysters begin to come back."

He slowed the boat again so Gus could get a good look at the riverbank. "Like I said, the state, the Coastal Resources folks, they're all fine with the idea of oyster farming," he said. "The towns are the problem."

"Little Penwick doesn't want oysters?" Gus said.

"It's the damn property owners," Benson said. "They don't want anything detracting from their beautiful views."

"I thought oysters lived underwater," Gus said,

"They do," Benson nodded. "But in artificial farming areas, they put the little baby oysters in cages just under the surface and expose them to the proper growing conditions, so they can grow up to be big and fat, get top dollar at the restaurants over in Newport, or up in Providence. And the people who own homes up there—" He pointed to some rooflines poking above the trees a hundred yards off the beachfront— "They say they swim and kayak and boat and fish in these waters and they don't want to look at the oyster farms or be bothered by having to steer around a few rows of cages."

Gus looked around. "I don't see anybody out here," he said. "No boats, no swimmers, no kayaks."

"Yeah," Benson said. "There never are. But those homeowners vote. And pay taxes. A lot of taxes. So the towns are fighting the farms. Too bad. It could be a great new industry for the state and it's good for the river. All hail the power of NIMBY—not in my back yard."

He cranked up the outboards and headed south again. Gus could now see the long granite block seawall that formed one of the boundaries of the Little Penwick harbor, and the buildings collected behind it. Beyond the seawall was the flat line of the ocean horizon, stretching out endlessly. Then he noticed a long wooden jetty spearing out into the river a few hundred yards north of the harbor entrance.

He pointed to it. "Whose jetty is that?" he asked Benson. "I thought the Coastal Resources people didn't allow long docks in the river."

Benson chuckled. "That one got grandfathered in," he said. "Been there at least a hundred years. Probably used by the rum runners during Prohibition." He turned the wheel and headed for the jetty. It extended out into the river for about a hundred yards, held up by thick pine posts that had been hammered into the muddy bottom every ten feet or so. About halfway out, there was a rickety wooden shed and they could see someone sitting in a chair outside the shed.

"Who owns that place?" Gus asked.

Benson smiled. "You don't know?" he asked, sounding surprised. "I think that's him now. I'll introduce you."

As the boat neared the jetty, where the shed was, Gus could see a man sitting in a white Adirondack chair. He was strumming on an acoustic guitar. Benson pulled the Zodiac up to the jetty, then cut the engines, stepped outside the cabin and dropped a spring line from midships around one of the wooden posts. The man strumming the guitar stopped and stood up.

"Hullo, gents," he said. "Beautiful day, innit?" The accent was veddy British. He smiled down at them. Then he blinked, twice. "Is that you, Officer Benson?" he said. "Haven't see you in donkey's years, mate. How're you gettin' on then?"

Gus felt his jaw drop. The man standing there was none other than Slate Evans, the legendary lead guitarist for the rock band The Slayers. The band had been one of many British groups that enjoyed its heyday back in the Sixties and Seventies, and had produced so many Grammy winning songs and albums that they almost had to retire the awards. The Slayers, most of whose members had somehow managed to survive the era of hard drugs, sex and rock'n'roll—although there had been a couple of casualties over the years—still toured the world to adoring crowds in sold-out stadiums and arenas, despite the fact that most of the musicians were well into their sixties now. Or seventies.

But Slate Evans was an icon in the world of rock. First for his amazing guitar riffs and solos, which teen-aged guitarists still tried to copy, but also for his legendary and apparently eternal agelessness. As Slate himself liked to boast, he had taken all the same drugs that had killed Hendrix and Joplin and Morrison and countless others, yet here he was, still on this side of the grass. The Internet was full of memes about the indestructible Slate Evans. How he used to have dinosaurs as pets. Or asking what kind of world our children will leave behind … for the ageless Slate Evans to enjoy. Or that only two things would survive a nuclear holocaust: cockroaches and Slate Evans.

Gus studied the man. He was rail thin, with long tattooed arms extending out from a sleeveless sweatshirt. His riven face was an amazing collection of crevices, deeply lined around his mouth, down his cheeks and across his brows. His hair was mostly gray, medium length, held away from his forehead with a bandana tied at the back, the strands fizzing up and out in all directions. There was a gold earring in his ear. He was barefoot and wore jeans that were weathered and torn. A cigarette hung from one corner of his mouth, smoky entrails casually floating up and over his head. But his sharp brown eyes were alert, taking in everything around him.

"Hiya, Slate," Benson said. "Sittin' by the dock of the bay, huh? You been in town for long?"

"Been here since Tuesday, mate," Evans said, taking a drag from his cigarette and tossing it into the water. He was apparently not worried about transgressing the laws against littering. "We finished a gig in Tokyo and I got nothing on the schedule again until August. So I'm here for a little hols, soaking up the sun."

"Slate, this is Gus Haddock," Benson said, motioning at Gus. "He's the chief of police here in Little Penwick. Thought you guys should know each other."

"Chief Haddock," Evans nodded at Gus, his alert, limpid eyes studying the man. "Wonderful name. Makes me hungry for some fish 'n' chips. Welcome to me 'umble abode." He bowed from the waist and gestured with the hand not holding the guitar at the mansion at the end of the jetty.

Gus looked down the jetty at the massive house. It had two wings extending out from the tall center, like arms wrapping around the expansive courtyard overlooking the river and the open ocean beyond. There were windows everywhere, a steep slate roof and a cupola at the top, with a brass weathervane extending above the rounded roof.

Everyone in Little Penwick knew that this rock star loved to come to town for a few weeks every summer, when his busy performing schedule allowed. He generally kept to himself, although he had been spotted around town from time to time, visiting one of the farm stands on Main Road, stopping in with music industry friends for a long boozy lunch at the Roadhouse, or walking, usually early in the morning, along Crescent Beach on the other side of town. But most of the people in town respected his privacy. Gus knew the department would occasionally get calls from Slate's neighbors reporting strange people massed outside his tall metal gates, or worse, trying to scale them in search of an autograph or just a Slate sighting.

"Big house for one dude," Gus said. "You don't get lonely in there by yourself?"

Slate Evans looked down at Gus, a smile playing on his lips.

"I wish I could feel lonely here, mate," he said. "House is always full. My record company invites various people to come stay with me. Guys from other bands. Gals from other bands. I think my cook told me this morning that she's got twenty-two for dinner tonight. Twenty effing two!"

He laughed and shook his head, amused at the absurdity of it all.

"Would you like a tour of the place?" Slate asked. "There's a bit of history to it."

Gus looked at Jack Benson, who shrugged. *Why not?* Benson cut the engines and quickly tied the boat securely to the dock. He and Gus clambered out.

Gus noticed two large men running through the manicured grounds overlooking the river and ocean and heading toward the dock. They were both dressed all in black, and looked like they both spent a lot of time at the gym, pumping weights. One was talking into a walkie-talkie.

"Oh, dear," Slate said as they began to walk up the jetty back towards the shore. "Here come the gendarmes. King and Kong. I apologize in advance. My record company insists I keep them on site. For my ..." he coughed, "*personal* safety."

The men in black waited until the group reached the end of the dock.

"I'm sorry, gentlemen," one of the black-clad men said. "This is private property. We're going to ask you to go back to your boat and leave at once."

Slate Evans waved a bony arm at the man. "Down, Kong, down," he said. "Me friends have come for a visit. It's not polite to chase them off." He pointed at Gus. "That one is our local chief of police," he said. "So I think my safety is not at risk."

Gus had his badge out and showed it to the guard Evans called Kong. "Officer Benson and I just stopped by to say hello," he said. "Mr. Evans has graciously invited us ashore."

Kong studied the two with narrowed eyes. His partner, King, spoke up.

"Welcome to Seaview," he said.

Slate handed King his guitar. "Good on ya, King," he said. "Would you take this back to the music room, please? Ta."

King didn't look all that pleased, but he took the guitar, motioned to Kong, and they backed away.

Evans led Gus and Benson up a stone staircase from the dock. To the left was a small narrow beach, maybe twenty yards long. Some kayaks and paddleboats were stacked in a wooden shed next to the beach. The stairs led to a series of patios, each on a slightly different level, that cascaded down from the mansion to the river. The level they stood on, just off the staircase, was full of chaises and tables shielded from the sun with umbrellas. Gus figured they would call this the sun deck, next to the beach. A bit higher up, and offset a bit to the right, was a swimming pool, long and narrow and made for swimming laps, with a pool house at the far end. There were more chaises next to the pool and the pool house had a long counter on one side. Behind the counter Gus could see a kitchen area with a large stainless steel refrigerator. He imagined there were rest rooms off the back.

They climbed up to the top level, which covered the expansive space between the two wings of the mansion that enveloped the patio area. Here there were formal gardens with groupings of annuals, shrubs and other plantings, low marble walls, sidewalks through grassy sections and sitting areas and a six-sided gazebo perched on a base providing lovely views back down the hill to the river and the Atlantic beyond. The ocean breeze wafted up the hill and provided a pleasantly cool counter to the warm sun.

"Place was built by one of the Vanderbilts," Slate Evans said as they took in the view of the gardens. "One of the minor ones. I think he owned a railroad between Louisville and St. Louis. He was only semi-rich, unlike the other Vanderbilts who built their cottages over in Newport." Slate nodded to the west. "So he built his place here. They said no one from society would ever come over to Little Penwick to visit him. So he imported his own party. That's why the house has twenty-one bedrooms."

"So this place was party central from the beginning," Benson said.

"And the party hasn't stopped since the day it was built," Slate said with a lopsided grin. "I'm just doin' my part to keep the tradition alive, yeah?"

Evans led them inside. Through the tall glass doors, they found themselves in a monumental formal ballroom, full of groupings of sofas, chairs and loveseats. The ceilings looked to be twenty feet high, the walls were covered in rococo gilded mirrors and painted frescoes showing medieval kings and queens, hillsides covered in wooly sheep and dark-eyed cattle and a grouping of dark portraits of unsmiling men, some in starched high collars.

"Your ancestors?" Gus said, nodding at the portraits.

Evans chortled. "Me Mum and Da were from East London," he said. "As were their Mums and Das, back as far as anyone knows. Dunno who these gents are. Must be old Vanderbilts."

He showed them the formal dining room, in another high-ceilinged section off on one side. The dark mahogany table that ran down the center of the room looked to be about forty feet long, and two chandeliers, with tiers of crystal pendants hanging down, hung above the table on long cables that dropped from the high ceiling. Sideboards were crammed with china and crystal glassware.

"Looks like you could have a hundred and twenty-two over for dinner," Benson said.

"Yeah," Evans said, sounding a little glum. "I might have to sneak out tonight and get me a burger instead."

Slate took them to see his music room, in one of the side wings. There was a bank of windows that looked out onto the river, but the walls were crammed with Marshall amps and other music-making gear. A glistening Steinway grand sat in the middle of the room, next to a full drum kit, stands holding guitars and basses, a few black music stands amid scatterings of chairs.

"You recording your next album in here?" Gus asked. "Looks like you're ready to go."

"Nah," Evans was shaking his head. "Actually the acoustics suck in here. I've been trying to get them to put some acoustic tiles on the ceiling, but me wife Gemma said that would ruin the historic aspects of the room, or some damn thing like that." He smiled. "The minor Vanderbilt used this room to seduce the young women who came to his endless parties. "I told Gemma that to be historically accurate, we should have vases full of condoms in this room. Hah!"

Benson and Gus smiled. Evans showed them his media room, with one of the largest TV screens Gus had ever seen, dominating one wall, and then led them into the front foyer, off the main entrance. A sweeping marble staircase rose for ten steps, then split into two and continued up to the second floor.

"Most of the bedrooms are up there," Evans glanced up the stairs. "But I won't bore you with all that. You seen one bedroom, you've about seen them all, right?"

Instead, he took them through a series of rooms and opened a door that led into his garage. There were six cars parked on the pristine cement floor. Gus saw two Mercedes sedans, a fire engine red Ferrari, a couple of Harley Davidson hogs, and three black SUVs at the far end.

"This is my toy room," he said. "Love to get me Harley out, now that it's warm. Hope you won't pull me over, Chief Haddock."

"Long as you keep to the speed limit, you should be fine," Gus said.

"Spoken like the copper that you are," Slate said, grinning.

He took them down into the basement, where the huge commercial kitchen was located. There were three chefs working at preparing lunch, which, Evans noted, was to be served in forty minutes.

"You gents want to stay?" he asked.

"Thanks, Slate, but I've got work I need to get back to," Gus said. "They're probably wondering where the hell I am right now. I told them I was going out with Officer Benson here, but didn't tell them for how long."

"Unnerstood," Slate said. "How 'bout a coffee instead?" He called to one of the chefs working nearby. "Hey, Katie … got anything for our friendly law enforcement types?"

Katie pushed back her bangs. Her face was flushed with working in the warm kitchen, despite all the air conditioning that was beamed into the room.

"Got some pastries that came in from Alma's Bakery," she said. "Would that do?"

"Anything from Alma's would be excellent," Gus said.

"No arguments from me," Jack Benson agreed.

"Lovely," Evans said. "Can you put together a plate, with three coffees, please Katie?" he said. "Have someone bring them up to the gazebo, would'ya? Ta, darlin'"

A few minutes later, the three were sitting around a table in the gazebo, staring out at the ocean and eating some cinnamon rolls while sipping coffee out of elegant china cups.

"I get the impression that you have a pretty large operation running this place," Gus said.

"Oh, yeah," Evans nodded, his mouth full of bun. "Prolly thirty, thirty-five people work here when I'm around."

"Where do they go when you go back on tour?" Benson asked.

Evans shrugged. "Some go back to my place in Connecticut," he said. "Others work for me over in London. I have a flat in West Brompton. Not far from the Chelsea football stadium. You like football?"

Gus smiled. "You mean soccer?"

"Soccer me ass," Evans said. "I mean good old English football, mate. The beautiful game."

"I find it mostly boring," Gus said.

Slate looked at him. "You should come to a game with me, mate," he said. "First we'll hit some of the local pubs and all. You know the Troubadour Cafe? Dylan did his first gig in England there. I live two blocks away. Then we'd take in the game, then go outside and crack some heads of the lads from the other side. Great good fun, it is."

Gus smiled. "Sounds like a wild time."

Evans looked at Gus, eyes narrowed. "Life is short, my man," he said. "If you don't live life to the full, make all of life a wild time, you're missing out. Grab it by the goolies and never let go." He clenched a fist in demonstration and shook it.

"Sounds like a motto to live by," Gus said. He glanced at his watch. "Thanks so much for the tour, the coffee and the rolls. But we need to get going. Duty calls."

"And you must answer the call," Evans said. "Come back any time, Chief. You too, Officer Benson. You lads are welcome here anytime."

A FEW MINUTES later, Gus and Benson were motoring away from the jetty. Benson headed back upriver and opened up the outboards. The Zodiac skimmed over the waves.

"Seems like a nice bloke," Gus said, as the mansion slowly disappeared in their wake.

Benson nodded. "He's just the same as the rest of us," he said. "Except a lot richer. And better at playing the guitar."

CHAPTER 8

AFTER PICKING UP his car at the marina in Portsmouth, Gus drove back to Little Penwick. When he walked into the station, he saw Buzz huddling with Jessica back in her office beyond the bullpen, so he went back to talk to them.

"What's up?" he said when he walked into Jessica's office.

"How was your weekend, chief?" Buzz said, a smile playing on his lips. "You get lucky?"

"Mighta hit the jackpot," was all Gus said in return. Jessica saw that Gus didn't want to play locker-room talk, so she jumped right in.

"We've checked with all the local banks," she told Gus. "As we all suspected, there are no accounts in the name of Janine Stone. Of course, she could be using a phony name and phony identification, so we asked the banks to watch out for any unusual cash withdrawals in the next few weeks. They all said they'd let us know."

"Good," Gus nodded. "Did we get that photograph from Frechette?"

Buzz held up a print. "Right here," he said. "I've put one on every officer's desk and handed them to the second shift as they went out the door. The image is a little fuzzy, but you can make out most of her features."

"OK," Gus said. "What's next?"

Jessica spoke up. "Buzz and I were just brainstorming, trying to figure out how we could get inside the Ferro compound, look around," she said. "We really need a mole over there, someone who can tell us where to look."

"What if we send someone up to Devens?" Gus said. "Talk to Danny Ferro himself."

"He's not going to tell you where he's hiding the money," Buzz said shaking his head. "He's probably thinking that cash will make a nice little nest egg once he gets out of the federal slammer. Even if that's still ten years from now. Six or seven with good behavior."

"What about his wife?" Gus prodded. "Maybe she knows where it is. Maybe she can be convinced to tell us something if we promise her a cut of the proceeds. I mean, she must be hurting for cash, with Danny on ice and Cosmo and the others up the river, too."

"I can pay a call on Catarina," Jessica said. "Maybe she'll talk to me, woman to woman."

"Do it," Gus said. "Soon as you can."

Buzz opened his mouth but before he could say anything, they all heard the sound of gunfire. Close. Followed by the whine of bullets flying in the air. They all flinched, shoulders hunched upwards, hands and arms protecting their heads. The sharp reports of the first shots was quickly followed by the sound of breaking glass. Jessica sat at her desk, as still as a marble statue. Buzz was ducking down behind the desk, head turned to look towards the front. Gus had turned and was striding towards the front of the station, where the shooting was coming from. His SIG Sauer was in his hand, and he didn't remember pulling it out of his holster. He counted at least ten shots, maybe more. They all heard Carl Lincoln, the officer of the day on duty at the front window to the station, mutter *son-of-a-bitch* and Gus saw him spin away from the window, desk chair flying backwards, his hand pressed up to his forehead.

"Dottie!" Gus yelled down the hall, "10-99, shots fired! 10-33, Urgent. All personnel return to base. Now!"

He ran over to Lincoln, who was still had his hand pressed up against his forehead. "Let me see, Carl, let me see," he yelled at his officer. Lincoln reluctantly pulled his hand away from his head. Gus could see that one of the bullets had grazed his officer's head, just below his hair line.

"You're OK," he said to the man. "You must have ducked at just the right moment. Just a graze. Barely broke the skin. Not even much blood." Carl nodded, but looked dazed by his close call.

Buzz appeared at his side, carrying a first aid kit. There were several around the office. Buzz guided Lincoln into the nearest chair, pulled out a wad of gauze and held it to Carl's head. "Nice going," he told the officer, "You just earned a Purple Heart."

Lincoln looked sideways at the detective. "Uh, Buzz, they don't have those for policemen."

"Oh," Buzz replied, daubing at the man's head with some disinfectant. "That's too bad. You should get the police union to demand one."

"Yeah," Lincoln said, "I'll get right on that."

Gus ran to the front door. The entryway between the glass doors to the outside and the Plexi window where visitors spoke to the office of the day was full of broken shards of glass. Whoever had fired at them had first blasted the doorway open and then sent a few final bullets into the interior. One had pierced either the Plexi or the thin sheet rock wall and nicked Lincoln.

Gus stuck his head out the now gaping opening in the front of the building. There was no one there. He looked both ways on Commerce Drive. Nothing. There was a small area along the road front where an area of decorative plantings surrounded the big wooden sign that announced Little Penwick Public Service Complex. The planted area was surrounded by a low rounded curb of asphalt. Gus could see that the car which apparently held the attackers had cut across a corner of the planted area. There was a tire track in the mulch there.

One of the town's police cars came screaming around the corner from the village green, sirens blaring. Jerry Hanlon pulled up and jumped out of his car.

"What happened, chief?" he yelled. "Got a 10-99 from Dottie."

Gus pointed at the broken front entrance, glass lying everywhere. "Somebody shot up the door," he said. "You see anyone leaving here at high speed?"

Hanlon shook his head. "Naw. Anybody inside hurt?"

"No, thank goodness," Gus said. "Carl was on duty at the front. He got nicked by a bullet. Superficial. He'll be fine." He paused. "We need to set up a crime scene out here. Park the car and string some tape. There should be some brass lying around. You know the drill."

"Got it chief," Hanlon said.

While he was moving his car, another came roaring into the lot. This time, it was Jamie McMaster, who pulled up next to Gus. After another quick recap, Gus sent Jamie to patrol down Easterly Road and to the highway on the east side of town.

"We're not sure what model we're looking for yet," Gus told the patrolman. "Look for anything suspicious. We'll radio any further details as we get them."

McMaster took off.

Gus went back into the station. Jessica had called for the EMTs next door to come over and look at Carl Lincoln. Two of them were affixing a bandage on his forehead. Jessica was standing in the middle of the bullpen, calling out orders. Buzz Franklin was at his desk, working at something on his computer, his face frozen in concentration.

"Buzz is calling up the video from the security system," Jessica told Gus. "We've got a camera on the front door and another on the parking lot. Hopefully we can see what kind of vehicle they were driving."

"Any idea of the make or model of the gun?" Gus asked. "Did we recover any spent rounds?"

"We'll start digging them out of the sheet rock soon," Jessica told him. "Did you see any brass left in the parking lot?"

"Jerry Hanlon is setting up a perimeter," Gus said. He thought of something.

"Call your contacts at the banks back," he said. "See if you can get them to give you any security video they have from their ATM machines. There's a chance one of those machines might have caught a view of the shooter's vehicle driving past."

Jessica nodded and started toward her desk. She stopped and looked at Gus.

"That's a new one," she said. "Where did you hear about that?"

Gus grinned at her. "I saw it on an old episdoe of NCIS I was watching last week," he said. "Have no idea if it's realistic or something the Hollywood guys made up."

Jessica nodded. "Worth a shot," she said. She went to her desk and began making calls.

Dottie Adams came out of her office. "Chief, Bob Murtha is on the line from city hall," she said. "He wants to know what the hell is going on."

"Tell him I'll call him back in a few," Gus ordered. "You can tell him the basics. But we're in full investigation mode, people. Let's find out the facts. What do we know. What do we not know."

Buzz called out from his desk. "Got it!" he yelled. Gus went over and stood behind him. Buzz punched a few buttons and after a brief pause when they could see nothing but gray noise, the front entrance to the department appeared on his computer screen. It showed the glass door with the black-and-gold decal of the Little Penwick Police Department on the top of the door panel. Then there was the sound of the gunshots, sharp snapping noises. The glass in the door and the adjoining panels to each side began to shatter and crash to the ground.

A few more shots followed. Then there was the sound of a vehicle accelerating, tires squealing in protest.

"We got the wider view?" Gus asked.

"Hang on a sec," Buzz said, pushing a few more keys on his keyboard.

The picture changed. This time, it showed an elevated view of the parking area in front of the entrance. There were no cars parked in front. They all watched as a large SUV entered the picture from the right, stopping in front of the glass doors. The windows were tinted and it was impossible to see the faces of the people in the SUV clearly…they were just shapes, dark ghosts. The shooter had been on the passenger side, and they watched as he stuck the gun out of the open window in the car and began firing. The barrel of the rifle flared brightly as the glass in the door shattered and fell, and the gunman added the last five or six shots into the now open foyer. Almost simultaneously to the last shot, the driver accelerated and the SUV disappeared out of the left frame of the shot.

"Looks like an Acadia," Buzz mused, as he reran the tape to look at the car again. "GMC. Mid-sized model. They come in dark gray, almost black and a dark hunter green."

"Can we see the plates from either angle?" Gus asked.

"Don't think so, chief," Buzz said. "I can look at the fire department cameras, see if they have a different angle."

"Right," Gus said. He turned to Dottie Adams, who was standing in the bullpen with everyone else. "Dottie—tell Jerry and Jamie they're looking for a dark colored GMC Acadia, black or green. That'll help them narrow it down. Then get on the horn and get everyone in here right away. All hands."

"Got it," she said and hightailed it back to her dispatch room.

Gus turned to Jessica. "Get an APB out on the car, Jess," he said. "We need to find it fast, before they dump it somewhere."

She nodded, phone already stuck in her ear. Gus went into his office and called Murtha at City Hall.

"What in tarnation is going on, chief?" the council president wanted to know.

"Somebody just shot up the front of our department," Gus told the man. "Blew out our glass doorway. Stray bullet creased the forehead of Carl Lincoln, but it was hardly even a flesh wound. EMTs put a bandaid on it. He's fine, back at work."

"Geez," Murtha said. "Any idea who did it?"

"Not yet, Bob," Gus said. "It just happened a few minutes ago. But we're all on it. I'll let you know soon as we know anything."

"OK, Gus," the man said, "But listen …"

Gus hung up the phone. He didn't have time for politics right now.

Jessica stuck her head in the chief's door. "Got the APB out, chief," she said. "Every police department in Rhode Island and six towns in Massachusetts are looking for it. I also requested any video from the Sakonnet Bank over on Willow. The shooter'd have to drive right by the bank to get here." She stopped and looked at him. "You feeling OK, Gus? No aftereffects?"

He wasn't sure if she was talking about his recent injuries from his encounter with the car from the other day, or about his PTSD from serving in the Mideast wars.

"You know," he said now, "I actually feel pretty good. Almost human again."

"Adrenaline," she said with a laugh. "Amazing stuff."

CHAPTER 9

WITH EVERYONE BENT to their tasks, the excitement level decreased. Now that they knew they were looking for a late model GMC Acadia, Gus was able to deploy his officers around town to look for it. Hanlon and Carl Lincoln photographed the parking lot, including three brass casings from the shooting that had apparently fallen outside the car's windows, and were working together to find and remove stray slugs from the wall. Jessica and Buzz Franklin were on the phones.

Bob Murtha came over from City Hall to survey the damage, and Gus showed him around, pointing out what they believed had happened. Murtha looked shaken.

"Do you think it was terrorists?" he asked.

Gus managed to keep from laughing as he shook his head. "Doubt it, Bob," he said. "They usually prefer bombs to spraying bullets at glass doors."

Murtha did a double take. "Are you taking this seriously?" he asked, "because I sure as hell am."

"We've launched an investigation," Gus told the council president. "We're gathering what facts we can. We expect to gather more in the next 12 to 24 hours. We will find whoever did this, and arrest them."

Murtha looked at Gus, looked into his eyes, then nodded. "Okay, chief," he said. "I'll get out of your way and leave you to it. Please keep me posted."

Murtha left the station as the truck from Sakonnet Glass pulled in. The two workers got out of their truck, looked at the damage, shook their heads and whistled.

"Man, you pissed someone off," one of the guys said.

"We need a new front door," Gus said. "How fast can we get one?"

The second worker had his tape measure out already. "We can replace the door panels right away," he said. "Got them in stock. But these side panels are special order. Probably take a few days. We'll put in a temporary patch with plywood. Won't look very nice, but it'll do the job."

"If it's only for a few days, then fine," Gus said. "Do it."

Measurements taken, they got back in their truck and drove away.

Now that the excitement had died away, Gus felt his knee begin to ache again. He hadn't used his crutch much, if at all, and now was beginning to feel it. He went back into his office and gulped down a pain pill. He knew it would be several hours before he could call it a day and go home.

GUS MADE IT a point to be in attendance at the next morning's roll call. The glass from the shooting had all been swept up, the door was operational again and the plywood side-panels made the entrance foyer much darker. He impressed on the day watch to keep an eye peeled for any dark colored SUVs and warned them that the perpetrators were to be considered armed and dangerous.

Jessica Martin also came in early. She told Gus that the APB had come up empty—none of the surrounding towns' police had seen the vehicle. She also said she was expecting to get some videotape from the Sakonnet Bank's ATM machine later that day. "They had to jump through some legal hoops," she said. "But they're sending over what they have."

"Good," Gus said, and went back into his office. He grimaced at the sight of his overflowing In box, armed himself with a cup of coffee and bent to work. An hour or two later he was making progress at clearing away the stack of papers on his desk when his father walked into his office. Julius Haddock had been chief of police for twenty-six years before Gus. Then he had been sent to jail by Attorney General Preston Knox. Before Gus and the Little Penwick PD had broken up the smuggling ring devised by Janine Stone and operated by the local Ferro family on behalf of the Providence mob. Which had paid Preston Knox to run interference for them. But Janine Stone had escaped and now Preston Knox was running for governor.

"Hey Dad," Gus said, signing a requisition form and tossing it into his Out box.

"Junior," Julius replied, sitting down in a guest chair. "Looks like you've had some excitement around here."

"What gave it away?" Gus said, smiling. "The deep shadows under my eyes or the plywood in the front door?"

"Might'a been everyone in town calling me to ask if I knew that the damn Al Qaedas attacked us yesterday in broad daylight," Julius said. "I had to talk a couple people down off the edge. They had their shotguns out and primed, ready to go hunt some filthy Ay-rabs up on Main Road."

"Well, thanks for that," Gus said. "I suspect we're gonna find the shooter is from closer to home."

"You got anything yet?" Julius asked. He knew the drill.

Gus shook his head. "Nope. Two guys in a late model GMC Acadia. Couldn't see the plates. Drove in, shot the hell out of the door, drove off, disappeared. You know anyone owns an Acadia?"

Julius shook his head. "Don't think so," he said. "Least, no one who wants to shoot up the cop shop."

Gus sat back in his chair and groaned a little. His father heard it and his ears perked up.

"What's wrong?" he asked. "You take a bullet in the shooting?"

Gus laughed a little. "Naw," he said. " I had a run-in with a car when I was out running a few days ago. Car won."

"Is that a fact?" Julius said, eyebrows raised. "So last week someone tries to run you over and this week someone shoots the glass out of your front door. I know I'm a retired lawman now who don't know crap, but as a private investigator I think that constitutes what we call a pattern."

"Only if both events were conducted by the same person or persons," Gus said. "And we don't know who conducted either one at the moment."

"What about Blondie?" Julius said.

Gus glanced at his father. "What makes you bring her up?" he said.

Julius shrugged. "Policeman's sixth sense," he said. "We've been waiting for her to drop the next shoe. Only a matter of time with someone like that."

Gus nodded. "Well, as a matter of fact, ICE told us that she's back in the country."

"Where'd she go?" his father asked, "On vacation?"

"South America," Gus told him. "And Mexico, they think."

Julius blew out some air. "You can take what ICE thinks and add five dollars and you'd maybe have enough for a cup of coffee. Maybe."

Gus shrugged. "Whatever," he said. "We're thinking she's back in town, maybe looking for some money someone owes her from last time. We proceeding on that assumption."

Julius nodded. "Sounds about right," he said. "That girl is pretty smart. And pretty tough. I wouldn't want to owe her any money, that's for sure."

He glanced at his watch. "Listen, I was thinking I'd take you to lunch, if you have time."

"I'd love to," Gus said. "But I need to pay a call on someone named O'Connell over at the Star Riders place. We've had some complaints about motorcycle noise."

"Oh, Christ," Julius said. "Agnes DeBoer is complaining again, isn't she? It's June and the weather is nice. That means the bikers are out in force and that means Agnes is calling in to complain. Happens every year." He laughed and shook his head. "I'll come with you, introduce you to the Big O."

"The Big O?"

"Ernie O'Connell," Julius said. "You'll like him. It's like time travel back to the Sixties with the Big O."

"Great," Gus said. He picked up his phone and called Dottie in dispatch to tell her he was going to lunch with his Dad with a stop first at the Star Riders Motorcycle club.

"Roger, chief," Dottie said. "And tell that old coot to stop in and see me after lunch. I miss him."

"Will do," Gus said.

They walked outside and got into Gus' police SUV, a dark navy blue Ford Navigator. Gus headed south on Commons Road, then cut over to the east onto Easterly, which ran south down to Crescent Beach.

"How's the private eye business?" Gus asked his father. "You were all over the news there for a while."

Julius chuckled. "Ever since we broke that cold case open a couple months ago, the phone's been ringing off the hook," he said. "And the letters ... dear God, I've got boxes of letters."

"Fan mail?"

"People wanting me to find their missing loved ones," Julius said. "I am now apparently the world's expert in solving thirty year old cases." He paused. "You ever hear of a place called Bonners Ferry?"

Gus paused, thinking. "Can't say that I have," he said.

"Me either," Julius said. "It's way up north in Idaho, up near the Canadian border. I got a letter from a lady in Bonners Ferry asking me to find out what happened to her husband. He left their house one afternoon twenty-two years ago, to run down to the market for a loaf of bread. Never came back.

No one's heard hide nor hair of him since. She thinks I can find him."

"Can you?" Gus said. "You did pretty good with Donna Dixon."

"Jesus Christ, son," Julius exploded. "That was a case right here in Little Penwick. Where I knew which people to call and what to ask. I don't know a goddam thing about Bonners Ferry and I wouldn't know which direction to start looking."

Gus chuckled. "So what are you doing with all the letters and phone calls?"

Julius sighed. "I got Siggi helping me," he said. "She's putting them into stacks and writing some kind of form letter to provide different answers, all of them adding up to a great big 'no.' She thinks I need to write them all back a personal letter. Do you know how much a goddam stamp costs these days? It'll cost me half a month's pension payment to respond to them all."

"Maybe you could make some money," Gus said, a smile playing on the corners of his lips. "Charge each one a nice fat retainer, up front. Have 'em sign a contract that says results not guaranteed. You could make a mint."

Julius Haddock looked at his son and shook his head. "Madness," he said.

Gus slowed down as they approached a huge maple tree by the side of the road. A small dirt lane cut to the east just past the tree, and Gus turned down it. The lane skirted a marshy patch on one side and a stand of new pines on the other and came out into a large clearing. It featured a grassless hardpan area beyond which stood a concrete block structure painted white, with a black door in the middle, and two windows on either side, framed by black shutters. A sign on the front read "Star Riders Motorcycle Club." There was a black star hung above the door.

"What's with the star thing?" Gus asked his father. He pulled up next to the door and killed the engine.

"This club was founded right after the Viet Nam War," Julius said, looking around at the empty clearing. "Most of the members back then were vets. The vets who came back slightly damaged. The ones who, after what they had seen and done over there, could not envision themselves joining polite society again, getting jobs as mechanics or boiler workers or landscapers. A lot of them ended up here. Bought a bike, drove it over here, went inside for some beer and sandwiches and talk about what they'd been through."

He got out, and bent over to pat the head of a German shepherd which came running around the side of the white block house and nuzzled Julius in the crotch.

"Place like this was like therapy for those guys," he said. "Kept a lot of them from going stark crazy. A lot of people in this town wanted me to run them out, give them the ole heave-ho. Bikers! Not normal people like we want in this town. But I wouldn't do it. They weren't doing nuthin' illegal. Oh, they drank pretty heavy here at times. Sometimes the music got a little loud. I felt it was good they had a place they could go and just be themselves. I took a lot of heat for that, but it was the right thing to do."

Gus got out and the dog came over to nuzzle him, too. He pushed the dog's head away, gently.

The black door opened and an old man came outside. He wore well-worn dungarees and a tattered T-shirt. He had long gray hair that he had pulled back and tied with a leather catch of some kind, so it cascaded down his back. He had bushy eyebrows, also mostly gray, a round face and bulbous nose and a long gray beard. One that reached almost down to his belt buckle. Looking at him, one would think he had once played bass for ZZ Top.

"Hey Julius," the man said to Gus' father. "Long time since you paid us a visit."

Julius stepped forward and the two men hugged, arms around shoulders. Julius stepped back.

"Ed," he said, "This is my son, Gus. He's the new chief of police. He said he needed to come over here and talk with you about something, so I volunteered to introduce you two."

Ed O'Connell stuck out his hand and Gus shook it. O'Connell held onto it and looked Gus right in the eyes.

"You were in the Rangers, right?" O'Connell said.

"I was," Gus said.

"Saw a little combat out there, did you?"

"More than I wanted to, for sure," Gus replied.

"Glad you made it back in one piece," O'Connell said. He let Gus' hand drop. "What can I do for you?"

Just then, there was a loud noise and all three men turned to look at the lane, where six bikes came hurtling out of the woods, circling in the clearing and pulling up to a stop next to Gus' police SUV. The noise of their exhaust was spectacular, Gus could feel it in his guts, and the bikes raised a cloud of dust that hovered in the air before the wind carried it off into the woods.

"We need to talk about noise," Gus said, nodding his head at the bikes that had just arrived. Three of the riders were solo, while the other three drivers had a woman perched on the back. They all got off, took off their helmets, unzipped their leathers, took off their gloves and smiled at each other with the kind of joy that only a biker understands.

O'Connell nodded at the new arrivals. "Beer's cold and Jenny's made some sandwiches," he told them. "C'mon in." He held the door open while the riders filed in, knocking fists with Ed and casting curious glances at the police vehicle, and Gus in his informal chief's uniform.

Once they were inside, O'Connell nodded at their bikes.

"Three Harley hogs, two Triumph Bonnevilles and the one on the end there is an old Yamaha pocket rocket," he said. "They all make a pretty good sound on the open road."

"What?" Gus said. "Can't hear ya." But he smiled.

O'Connell looked at him for a moment, then grinned. "Chief with a sense of humor," he said. "Ain't all bad."

"I'm not trying to bust your balls, Ed," Gus said. "But I've had calls from the citizens complaining about the noise. Wondering if there's anything you can do to help tone it down a bit."

"It's that DeBoer woman, ain't it?" O'Connell said. "Man, she's like clockwork. Every June, she complains to the town about the noise. Like clockwork."

"I know," Gus nodded. "Sounds like she's a pain in the ass. On the other hand, there is a town ordinance says you can't blast around town willy nilly. I'm just here asking politely if you could speak to the members and ask if they could try and keep the noise level manageable. Maybe cut down a bit on the snapping, especially over near the beach. Make sure they got mufflers and that they're working properly. I really don't want to tell my men to start handing out citations."

"Appreciate that, Chief," O'Connell nodded. "We got a chapter meeting on Sunday. I'll make a note to tell the guys to try and avoid the road down to the beach for a while. Miss Agnes will calm down. She always does." He paused, then cocked his head. "Of course, we get a lot of out-of-towners down here in the summer, too. We have what they call reciprocal deals with other clubs around New England. Lot of 'em like to come down here in the summer. You can ride for forty miles along the coast if you know the way. Two lanes and mostly empty. They come down to enjoy our roads and the beaches and all. I can't guarantee I can get all of them to quiet down. But I'll try."

"Appreciate that, Ed, I really do," Gus said. He paused. "Where did you serve?"

O'Connell turned and looked at Gus. "I was in Nam," he said, "Right at the end. Got shot at once or twice, but I was never in the real shit storm. Helped evac a lotta fellas who were, though." He shook his head sadly and winced with the memory.

Gus nodded. Even across the generations that separated them, he and Ed had a connection. Band of brothers. That never left, never faded, no matter how many years had gone by.

"Thanks for helping," Gus said. "I appreciate it. A lot."

O'Connell nodded. He turned to Julius. "You come back and have a few brewskis with us, Chief. You're always welcome here."

"I'll do that, Big O," Julius said. They man-hugged again. "Real soon."

CHAPTER 10

THE NEXT MORNING, Gus drove up to Brockton, a decaying city within the suburban ring south of Boston, for his monthly appointment with Dr. Susan Maloney, a psychiatrist who specialized in dealing with PTSD issues among those working in law enforcement. Gus had been ordered to see her the previous fall when tensions had been high in his life: he was new at the job, his father was in jail, the Attorney General of Rhode Island had ordered a Special Master from his office to supervise the day-to-day operations of his department, and Gus was feeling everyone was out to get him. His three tours with the Army Rangers in heavy combat in Iraq and Afghanistan had been the excuse. PTSD. Everyone had it, even if they didn't know it.

All that had calmed down, but Gus had come to look forward to his monthly sessions in Dr. Maloney's quiet office. He liked talking with her and had to admit that her advice was always sound.

"Hello, Gus," Dr. Maloney greeting him when he walked in and sat down. Dr. Maloney did not believe in couches, so he sat in a comfortable visitor's chair in front of her desk. "How are things going?"

Gus sighed and looked at her. "Mayday," he said.

"Oh dear," the doctor said. "That doesn't sound very good. Would you care to elaborate?" She flipped the pages over in her notebook, leaving a nice, new, unwritten-upon sheet for her notes.

"Maggie is pregnant," he said. "She told me Friday night."

"I see," Dr. Maloney said. Her voice was even and her tone non-judgmental. Just what one would expect from a shrink. "How do you feel about that?"

"Surprised, of course," he said.

She nodded.

"Taken aback."

"That's mostly the same as surprised," she said.

"I guess a little resentful," he said. "Like the trap was sprung."

She nodded again, gazing at him steadily. "Okay," she said. "That's understandable. The news was unexpected. Out of left field. No warning. Just fait accompli."

"Yes," Gus said. "All of that."

"I can see how one would feel resentment at being told something as important, as weighty, as the news that a new life has been created," she said. "I assume you two talked about all this?"

"I asked her what happened," Gus said. "She didn't like that very much."

"No," the doctor said, "I can see how that might be upsetting to her. She tells you something important, indeed earth-shaking and, one assumes, news that she thinks is wonderful. And you respond by asking how in the hell this happened."

"Ouch," Gus said.

"But that is not to invalidate your feelings, either," she said. "I can also understand your reaction. You and Maggie are in a relationship, but, at least as far as I know, you two have not yet discussed … er … *formalizing* that relationship."

"Like, are we going to get married?" Gus said. "Where are we going to live? Who is going to take care of the baby, since we both have full-time jobs? Is this the right time for a baby? Did she want to do this? Am I just a sperm-donor who's supposed to be happy that I've now got a kid that I have to take care of for the next twenty odd years, or, really, for the rest of my life."

She paused, looking at him with what he hoped was kindness.

"I can hear that you are still a little miffed," she said. "Am I right?"

"Yes," he said. "Miffed is a good word. I mean, I love Maggie and don't want to stop seeing her. But this thing just dropped on my head. Boom. No warning. I'm still trying to figure out how I feel."

"Yes," she said. "I understand. You feel the way you do, and it's not unreasonable to feel that way. It is a kind of blindsiding. But, on the other hand, it's probably not entirely unexpected, is it?"

"Is this where the 'takes two to tango' thing comes up?" he said.

She smiled. "Yes," she said. "No matter what method of birth control you were using, there is a chance, small but not zero, that it won't work. So when you are in a relationship which includes having sex, there is an unspoken realization that every act of sexual congress could result in a pregnancy."

"So I shouldn't feel resentful," Gus said, frowning. He paused, thinking. "Sorry, but I do."

"And, again," she said, "I respect your feelings. The question is, how do we move beyond them?"

"Like, what do we do next?" Gus said.

"Yes," she said. "Like it or not, the die has been cast. If you want to feel resentment, that is your right. But that's not going to help both of you move forward. Maggie is, no doubt, feeling quite vulnerable right about now. She is carrying your child, like it or not, and wants to know what you're going to do about it."

"Not much I can do, is there, at this point?" Gus said.

"Of course there is," she said forcefully. She pointed her pen at him across the desk. "You have many options. Some are better than others. Some may hurt, or be hurtful. But there are many things you can do, many ways you can react."

Gus shook his head. He had been thinking about nothing but the options he had, and he didn't really like any of them.

"I'm not going to be an asshole," he said.

"Of course not," she said. "Because you are not one."

"I don't want her to get rid of it," he said next. "That just seems extreme to me."

She nodded, letting him think it through.

"I don't want to stop seeing Maggie, either," he said.

"Because …?"

"Because I love her," he said. "I love her being part of my life."

"Yes," the doctor said. "So …?"

"So I need to get over feeling resentment and deal with it," Gus said.

"Yes. And no," she said. "You will have to deal with your feelings. But you shouldn't have to deal with them by yourself. When you are in a committed relationship, and that's what I think you and Maggie are, you have to learn to share things. In this case, you need to find a way to share your feelings of resentment with her, and let her react. Then you deal with her reaction. And she deals with yours. And so on. None of that is easy. It all requires lots of communication and understanding. On both sides."

"What if her resentment of me leads her to end it?" he asked. "What if I've already screwed the pooch?"

"Then you have to figure out a way to deal with that," she said. "It would be quite a severe loss and that would require quite a bit of time. But I think you could do it, if it came to that. Plus, you have a secret weapon."

"I do?" Gus said. "What?"

She smiled. "Me," she said. She flipped her book to the calendar page. "I'll make your next appointment in a month. But if you need to come in before that, just give me a call. And if you think it might be helpful, ask Maggie if she wants to come with you. I can share some communication ideas, maybe referee a discussion. There are lots of ways to deal with this. You are not alone, Gus."

"I guess not," he said. He flexed his shoulders. "It just feels that way."

CHAPTER 11

AFTER LEAVING THE office of Dr. Maloney, Gus headed south before cutting west across southern Massachusetts into Rhode Island and Providence. He called Dottie Adams in dispatch and told her he was going to visit Maggie and would likely spend the night in Providence with her.

"Personal time," he said to her.

"You're the chief," she said. "You can pretty much do what you want."

"Right," he said and hung up.

His destination was the Olneyville neighborhood on Providence's west side. Olneyville is not one of the neighborhoods the Chamber of Commerce tells visitors not to miss in Providence. Hemmed in on one side by the busy Route 6, on the other by the busy Route 10 and on yet another side by the Woonasquatucket River, it's a workingman's neighborhood where nobody works anymore. Long streets of three-story wooden tenements end at decaying brick factories with tall brick smokestacks tell the story of a once-busy factory town. But the factories no longer make anything.

On the handful of busy commercial streets, city buses groan and belch exhaust as they pass by roofless decaying wooden buildings, many with plywood windows, and buildings decorated by the artistic graffiti offerings of one or another of the city's mostly Hispanic gangs. Olneyville is the personification of the Rust Belt, a once-thriving and hard working part of the city that is now decrepit, decayed and dying. If not already dead. It had once been the ticket to the middle class for the workers from Ireland, Italy, French Canada and elsewhere who lived there in its heyday. These days, one still finds lots of immigrants living in the dreary tenements, but they come from the Dominican Republic, Nicaragua, Haiti, Mexico and Viet Nam. Olneyville is one of Providence's go-to places for heroin, crack, fentanyl, prostitution, poverty and crime.

Naturally, that's where Maggie Wells' nonprofit organization, the Sunrise Center, had opened a storefront for battered and abused women. There were a lot of battered and abused customers to be found in Olneyville. Gus parked his police car next to a hydrant next to the Sunrise Center's front door, and walked inside. The Center's facade was made of wood, shiny with recently applied white paint, topped by a row of narrow windows. A sign affixed to the front wall showed a bright yellow sunburst illustration along with the name of the place and a phone number.

Inside the heavy wooden door, Gus encountered an older black man reading a book, sitting behind a card table, dressed in jeans and a T-shirt, with a pencil stuck behind his ear, partially hiding in a frizzy gray Afro. The man stood up from a folding metal chair as if to challenge Gus, but then he noticed the police uniform Gus was wearing, and, with a nod, he sat back down.

There was a large room to the left with a sofa, a couple of upholstered chairs, a low cocktail table and several more metal folding chairs. There were maybe ten or twelve women sitting in these chairs. It looked like a group meeting of some kind. Several of the women held cardboard coffee cups and two of them were smoking cigarettes, probably in defiance of the state's ban on indoor smoking. They did not look like they cared what the state thought of their behavior. All of the women looked up when he came in and most of them were still looking at him with various expressions of challenge, or fear, except for a few who kept their faces blank.

Maggie Wells walked out of an office in the back, through a wooden door. She was accompanied by a young black woman in a denim dress, who was holding the hand of her daughter, who looked to be about three years old, her curly black hair collected in ringlets and tied up with colorful ribbons of pink and yellow. The little girl looked at Gus and smiled.

Maggie saw Gus and her eyes lit up, as if she was happy to see him. Then, as he watched, a shadow fell and she looked away, uncertain, uncomfortable. Gus felt his throat constrict. He wondered, for a moment, if he was too late.

"Gus," she said, coming over and giving him a quick hug. "What brings you up to the big city?"

He was about to tell her when the door to the street was pushed open and a tall, thin black man came in. He had a cleanly shaven head, a gold earring in one ear, and several layers of gold and silver chains around his neck. He was dressed in jeans, a T-shirt and new-looking trainers. He looked around the large front room, scowling. The scowl was just one give-away—everything about the man gave off vibrations of anger and impatience.

The older man sitting at the card table just inside the door stood up again and held his hands out.

"Ah'm sorry, DeShawn, but you cain't come in here," he said to the younger man. "You been told not to come up here."

"I'm here to see my bitch," the younger man said, his voice raised. "She my bitch. She belong to me. I gonna see her. I gonna take her home w'me."

"I ain't yo bitch, motherfucker," said one of the women sitting on the old sofa. She was a large woman, with slicked hair pulled tight against her skull, dressed in a T-shirt and a pair of white pants. "And I ain't comin' home wid you. Not now. Not evah."

The security guard moved around to his right to get between the man and the women in the long room. DeShawn tried to move around him, and they did a little dance, back and forth for a count or two. Finally, the younger man had enough.

"Get yo black ass the hell outta my way," he said and he pushed the older man hard, making him stumble backwards a step or two. He pointed at the woman on the couch. "And you get yo' black ass out dat door, bitch. I ain't sayin' it twice."

He took a threatening step towards her. Gus, who had been standing off to one side, next to Maggie and the woman with the little girl who had come out of Maggie's office, stepped forward and halted the man's forward progress.

"Excuse me, sir," Gus said to the man, holding his hands out in a hold-up manner.. "But I'm going to ask you to come outside with me. We can talk about this, but we're going to talk outside, on the sidewalk."

"Whatchoo talkin' 'bout, cracker?" the man said. "I ain't goin' nowhere 'ceptin back to my crib. Wid that bitch ovah there." He nodded at the large woman on the couch. "You get me?"

He raised his left arm to point at the woman on the couch. When he did, Gus grabbed him by the wrist, bent his arm back and around and pulled it up his back until it almost reached his neck.

"Owww," the man howled, "Let me go, honky man."

"Outside," Gus growled at him.

The man started to resist, trying to break away from the hold Gus had on his arm. Gus turned him toward the front door and pushed him forward, hard. The man stumbled forward. Gus dipped his shoulder and put it in the man's back and shoved him face first into the door. Everyone in the room heard the sickening dull thump of the man's skull connecting with the hardwood door.

"Owww," the man howled again. "You broke my haid, motherfucker. Get off'a me."

"Gus!" Maggie spoke sharply.

Gus reached around with his free hand and pulled the door open. Then he shoved the man out the door onto the sidewalk and followed him out. The security man came with them. Once on the sidewalk, Gus released the hold on the man's arm. He groaned and rubbed his shoulder with his other hand.

"You done broke mah haid," he muttered. "I gotta go up the hospital. Mah haid's done broke."

The older man pointed a finger at him. "DeShawn, you cain't come here no mo', you get that?" he said. "Angelique has got a court order sayin' you cain't be near her. You cain't see her. You cain't call her. You cain't talk to her. You gots to leave her be. And the judge say if you don't do that, he will send you to the jail. Now git yourself gone, boy. Final warning."

DeShawn was still moaning, rubbing his shoulder where Gus had stretched it, and feeling around on his forehead, looking to see if there was any blood. There wasn't. He glared at both of them.

"I comin' after both you," he said, his eyes red-rimmed and angry. "I comin' soon. Don' you forget me."

"You come back here and you'll be arrested," Gus said. "You've been enjoined by the court and you are not permitted to contact Angelique. You stay away from here. You stay away from Angelique. Or else you're going to be in a world of hurt. Don't you forget that, DeShawn."

"I get my posse and I get you dead, motherfucker," DeShawn said. "Don' care if you be poh-leece or not."

"Are you threatening me?" Gus said. "Please tell me you are threatening me. In front of this witness." He pointed at the older black man, who was standing to the side, watching.

"Ain't no threat," the black man said. "It be a fact, Jack." But he turned and started walking away down the sidewalk. Still rubbing his sore shoulder and looking back from time to time, muttering something only he could hear. Gus watched him until the man was a block away.

Gus turned to the older man. "He seems nice," Gus said. "You get a lot of that type around here?"

The older man chuckled and stuck out a hand. "Arthur Manville," he said. "'Preciate your help. That DeShawn been a thorn 'round here for a month or so now. His woman had enough of his jive, had enough of gettin' her ass beat on a nightly basis. Miss Maggie took her 'fore the judge and got a restraining order. He ain't taken kindly to that. At all."

"What will you do if he comes back?" Gus asked.

Arthur shrugged. "Call the cops," he said. "Not much else I can do, legal-wise. Miss Maggie knows all this, all the legal mumbo-jumbo, and tells me what I can and cain't do."

"Well, if you need reinforcements, give me a call," Gus said. "Be happy to knock some more sense into his thick head."

Arthur chuckled again and nodded. "Know what you mean," he said. "DeShawn one o' the bad ones. Not much one can do with the likes of him."

MAGGIE TOOK GUS to dinner at New Rivers, an intimate little bistro on Steeple Street, at the bottom of College Hill near the river where they staged the Waterfire concerts and spectacles on summer weekend nights. Steeple Street was aptly named as across North Main, the stepped tower of the First Baptist Church in America rose into the sky. While grandly named, it was also accurate: this was the church founded by the Rev. Roger Williams in the new colony he named Rhode Island

and Providence Plantations after the cheerless Puritans in Boston booted him out of their colony for being too Christian.

Gus had the bluefish fritters and a cold beer while Maggie nibbled at her caramelized fennel crepes. She poked at her plate as if she was distracted about something. Like, Gus surmised, being pregnant with his baby and not knowing what was going to happen with all that.

"Is there something the matter?" he asked when their dishes had been taken away. He knew that was the signal for her to begin complaining about whatever he had done, whether he had done it or not. But after his session with Dr. Maloney, he felt it was important that they keep talking.

"You went straight to the violence with DeShawn Taylor," she said, leveling her deep brown eyes at him. "There was not even a hint of negotiation or a suggestion to do this or else that. You just smashed his head against the door."

Gus was surprised, but tried not to show it. He figured this was her way of getting to the real matter at hand by a circuitous route. He'd play along.

"It's called 'getting their attention' in police lingo," Gus said, sipping the last of his beer. It was from a local small-batch bottler and it was quite tasty. He really wanted another, for several reasons, but thought better of that idea, especially since Maggie wasn't drinking. "Some people cannot be reasoned with. Nor bargained with. In my judgment, DeShawn was about to go straight to physically attacking his bitch. So I stopped that idea cold and dissuaded him."

Maggie was shaking her head. "I don't know," she said. "It seems to me that talking can often be …"

"A waste of a lot of time," Gus said. "Mags, I love you and I love what you do, but when it comes to the criminal part of the population, you've just got to trust me on this. Sometimes a smack upside the head is the only communication tool you've got. And you will notice that after I smacked him upside the head, he went outside with me and then he went away. The threat was ended."

"He said he was coming back with his posse," she said. "That sounds like a delayed threat, not an ended one."

He wanted to suggest that she was just being argumentative, but restrained himself. He had long ago learned not to get into a pissing fight with a lawyer, especially over issues of the law.

"Your security guy Arthur knows what to do if he shows up again," Gus said instead. "But I don't think he will. Guys like that always talk trash. It's part of their persona. You just nod and send them on their way. He doesn't want to spend time in the lockup. He was just testing the waters. Now he knows. You've got security and backup and you will call them if you need to. He'll wait and try to find Angelique someplace else, where she's more vulnerable."

"You think he'll do that?" Maggie said, looking at Gus with eyes that were suddenly fearful and concerned. "I need to tell her that."

Gus chuckled, softly. "I dunno," he said. "I've never talked to Angelique, but my guess is that she knows exactly what kind of dude DeShawn is. They've known each other for a while, no?"

Maggie nodded. "Long enough to have two kids with him," she said.

"See?" Gus said. "Your job is to keep telling her to stay away from him."

Maggie sighed. "That's so true," she said. "I can't remember how many of our clients have come in, gone through the initial stages of the program, and then gone straight back to their man, back to the conditions that drove them to us in the first place. It can be sooo depressing."

Gus nodded. "I know," he said. "It's the same with recidivist criminals, alcoholics, many others. They know they shouldn't do the thing that got them in trouble in the first place, but they can't help themselves. It's like they're drawn by some kind of spooky force field into doing it again. And again."

"So tell me what happened with this shooting," Maggie said, changing the subject. "Is everyone okay at the station?"

"Carl Lincoln has a minor scratch, but he was lucky," Gus said, frowning. "If what the shooter was doing was trying to leave us a message, he came pretty close to committing a homicide. That's the only scary part."

"Who do you think did it?" she asked.

Gus shrugged. "Dunno," he said. "But I'm guessing whoever it was, Janine Stone was in the background, encouraging it. It's got all her earmarks: loud, scary and un-ignorable."

"What is her message, though?"

"She's letting me know that she can operate in Little Penwick with impunity," Gus said. "Telling me that it might be my town, but she's somewhere in it. Like whoever it was who tried to run me over. It's all 'Look what I can do, copper.'"

"How do you answer that?"

Gus smiled. "I find her, I bust her and I send her away for a long time," he said. He pushed back from the table. "Whaddaya say we go for a walk along the river? It's a nice night out."

"Should you be walking with your knee and all?" Maggie asked.

"It's actually good to stretch it out some," Gus said. "I'll stop if it starts hurting again. Shall we go?"

Maggie smiled her assent and they walked outside into the gloaming of the evening. Rush hour traffic had died down and they could actually hear the wind ruffling the leaves on the trees that dotted the riverbank. He took her hand and they walked along the Woonasquatucket River, looking at the tall buildings of downtown, and the gold-domed centerpiece of the nearby state capitol.

"Did you know Woonasquatucket means 'where the salt water ends' in Algonquin?" Maggie said as they strolled.

"Did you study Algonquin in college?" Gus said. "Or did you learn that on the Internet?"

She bumped him with her hip. "Smartass," she said. But she said it with fondness.

They crossed over a bridge and walked back down the river in the other direction. Gus reached over and took her hand. He felt her react: muscles tensed, sharp intake of breath. But then she relaxed and squeezed his hand back.

He led her over to a bench where they could sit and look at the dark water and the tall buildings of downtown Providence behind. The sun was setting and the western sky was painted in streaks of pink and orange, the colors of sherbet. It was peaceful, if you ignored the sirens from a nearby squad car, rushing to the scene of a shooting or something.

"I feel like maybe I haven't reacted very well to the news," Gus said after they had settled in. "I'm sorry about that."

She still held his hand, and squeezed it again now.

"It's okay," she said. "It's big and important and came at you out of the blue. I can understand how you might feel overwhelmed. I feel like that, too. Like every hour of every day."

"I just had my monthly appointment with Dr. Maloney," he said.

"She shrink you?" Maggie said, smiling. "Or did she blame everything on me?"

"No blame," he said. "Not much shrinking, either. She just asks a lot of questions and lets me figure things out best I can."

"Have you figured us out yet?"

He smiled at her this time. "That could well prove to be a lifetime project," he said. "Figuring us out."

She turned and looked at him.

"Does that mean you want to try?"

He looked into her eyes. Fell into them, really. They were bottomless.

"Of course I do, Mags," he said. "That was never the question. I'm just trying to get my head around it all."

"I know," she said. "Me, too."

"We can do this, right?" he said. "The whole thing? Together?"

She didn't speak. She leaned in and kissed him on the lips, lightly.

"Together," she said. "Always."

IN THE MORNING, the buzzing of Gus' phone woke him out of a sound sleep just after seven. He glanced at the screen and saw that his chief of detectives, Buzz Franklin, was calling. The bed was empty. He could hear the shower running in the bathroom.

"What's up, Buzz?" he said. "And it better be good since it's early."

"Hey chief," Franklin said, trying, and failing, to disguise the amusement in his voice. "Not interrupting anything in your Providence love nest, am I?"

"You're interrupting me getting another hour of sleep," Gus replied. "What do you want?"

"We got the tapes from the Sakonnet Bank's ATM video," he said. "And son of a gun, there was a shot of the Acadia driving by in the background. I played with the images last night and finally got one that showed the passenger in the car."

"You know who it is?" Gus asked, his voice rising in excitement.

"You betcha," Buzz said. "And you'll be surprised to learn it is one of the Ferro clan."

Gus swung his legs out of the bed and stood up.

"No shit?" he said. "Tell me more."

"It's Jack Ferro," Buzz said. "One of Danny's cousins."

"Let's get a warrant and go out and talk to him," Gus said.

"Already done, boss," Franklin said. "The judge just faxed it over to me."

"Beautiful," Gus said. He thought for a minute. "I'll be down there in about an hour. We'll go pay him a visit."

"Ready when you are, chief," Buzz said. "Say hi to the lovely Maggie for me."

Maggie came out of the bathroom, her damp hair wrapped in a towel and not another stitch on her.

"Lovely doesn't even begin to get there," Gus said. "Let's make it two hours before I get back."

Buzz was laughing when Gus hung up the phone.

CHAPTER 12

Gus got back to Little Penwick around ten. He found Buzz Franklin sitting in his office off the bullpen, sipping on coffee and tapping away at his computer. Buzz looked up when Gus walked in.

"Tell me what you got," Gus said.

Buzz turned his computer around so Gus could see his screen.

"The bank's system is a slo-mo continuous loop," he explained. "It's designed to capture the faces of customers using the ATM machine. The bank's head of security told Jessica that's in case there's a dispute over a transaction, or in case someone comes up with a crowbar or something and tries to steal money from the machine. Anyway, they were able to isolate the parts of the tape just prior to the shooting here, and caught a pretty good side shot of the Acadia passing in front of the bank. It was the passenger side, so after zooming in and clearing it up, I was able to get a pretty good likeness of the passenger. His window was down, which helped a lot."

He clicked on a file and the screen showed a young man in a baseball cap sitting in the passenger seat in the front of the

Acadia. There was a long rounded shape that the man was holding in front.

"You can see the barrel of the rifle there," Buzz said, pointing to the shape. "Looks like he was getting it ready to point out the window when they got to the police station, which is just about four hundred yards from the bank."

"You're sure it's the Ferro boy?" Gus asked.

"Yup," Buzz nodded. "I blew it up and sharpened the pixels and got a good image. It's him."

"What do we know about Jack?" Gus asked next.

Buzz turned back to his computer, calling up another document. "I was just going over his record," Buzz said. "He's just turned twenty. Nothing serious in his background. At least, nothing felonious yet. Couple of speeding tickets and one warning for public nuisance. That last was two years ago. A little free-for-all at the high school in Portsmouth, after a football game."

"He got a job?"

Buzz shrugged. "He's done some work at a couple gas stations over on the Island," he said. "Pumping gas, changing oil, stuff like that. Now he's working as a clerk in a convenience store. No full time career that I can see."

"So he's just kinda bumping along," Gus said. "No real career, no more education. Waiting for trouble to find him."

Buzz nodded. "Sounds about right," he said. "It's kinda the Ferro family motto, isn't it? ... Waiting for trouble."

"You think he's home? Gus asked.

"Where else would he be?"

Gus nodded. "Let's go pick him up."

Both men checked their weapons to make sure their clips were full before replacing them on their hips. Franklin took the paperwork and they went outside.

"Let's take my car," Buzz said. "No sense announcing our presence by driving your marked squad car into the Ferro neighborhood."

They got into his dark blue unmarked Ford Taurus sedan and Buzz wheeled it out of the lot. It only took about five minutes to drive down the Easterly Road and turn onto the dirt and crushed shell private road that cut deep into the swampy interior before emerging onto the large open plain around which several of the Ferro family houses and trailers were positioned. Franklin drove past the big old white house with its wraparound porch that had once been the home of Angelo Ferro and then his son Danny, and where Janine Stone had lived for two or three years while she was cooking up her human smuggling network. Angelo was now somewhere at the bottom of the sea, and Danny was now at the federal prison in Devens, northeast of Boston, doing seven to fifteen years.

Buzz pulled to a stop in front of a light green trailer, parked on concrete blocks. There was a rusty aluminum awning over the door on the side, and a metal chimney poked above the roof on the far side of the trailer. That was likely the vent for Jack Ferro's wood-burning stove, which helped get him through the cold winter months. The metallic panels on the outside of the trailer were dirty and starting to rust at the seams. It looked like it had been years since the place had received any kind of maintenance.

Gus and Buzz got out of the sedan and Buzz pounded loudly on the front door. It made the door and the entire trailer shake.

"Police!" he called out. "Open up, Jack."

They could hear a muted groan from inside, followed by sounds of someone stirring. After a minute or so, the door opened and Jack Ferro peered out. He was tall, his face was covered with a couple days' worth growth of whiskers and his dark hair was long and on the greasy side. He was wearing an Army-green T-shirt and a pair of old jeans, but was barefoot. Jack was on the chunky side and his ample pinkish belly peeked out from beneath the bottom of his T-shirt. He blinked rapidly against the bright light of the day, looking like someone who had just been rousted our of bed.

"What the hell do you want?" Jack said, scratching the top of his head. "I'm trying to sleep here."

"You don't have a job to go to?" Buzz asked. "It's almost noon. You're gonna be late. Bosses don't like late."

Jack yawned, showing off his brown stained teeth, and a bit more of his belly fat. "I don't start my shift until four," he told them. "So quit the hassling and just tell me what you want."

Buzz held up the search warrant the judge had signed and faxed. "Got a warrant to search the premises," he told Jack. "Please step outside. Do you have any firearms in this residence?"

Jack had taken the warrant and was looking at it. He stopped reading it and looked up, confused.

"Wha-?" he said. "What did you ask me?"

"I asked you if there are any firearms in this residence," Buzz said. "Before we start searching the premises, we like to know what we might find, and we don't like surprises. So again, do you have any weapons we should know about?"

Jack looked at their faces, glanced down at the warrant, then looked up again.

"Ah, no, I don't think so," he said.

Gus and Buzzy looked at each other. *He's got guns* they both thought.

Buzz motioned to a rusty metal lawn chair set next to a fire pit ringed with stones. "Why don't you park it over there, Jackie," he said. "You enjoy this beautiful day and we'll do our thing and get out of your hair as fast as possible."

The young man looked like he wanted to protest, but he did what he was told and sat down.

Buzz held the door open and motioned for Gus to go ahead. They went inside the trailer. Both were struck by the odor of stale cigarettes and spilled beer. As in most trailers Gus had ever seen, the front door was located about a third of the way down the length of the trailer. To the right of the door, occupying the end section, was a very small galley kitchen with a single sink, two-burner electric hot plate, a microwave oven and, under the small counter, a half-size refrigerator.

As they entered, they were standing in the living room part of the trailer. About fifteen feet long, the round cast-iron stove sat against the far wall across from a built-in sofa which con-sisted of two lumpy looking upholstered cushions to sit on, and two more for backrests. A thin wall traversed the space beyond the sofa, with a door open in the middle that showed them Jack's bedroom. A very small bathroom, with enough room for a toilet and a stand-up shower, was squeezed in past the bedroom door.

There were a few small tables here and there, as well as a good-size flat screen television. Ashtrays on the tabletops were crammed full of expired butts and there were numerous empty and crushed cans of beer scattered around on the floor.

"Don't think Martha Stewart designed this place," Buzz said as they looked around. "Trailer trash chic."

"Hey!" came a protesting voice from outside. "I can hear you y'know."

Gus and Buzz looked at each other and smiled. Gus indicated that Buzz should start in the bedroom, while he turned to the kitchen end. They both put on mylar gloves for the search.

A quick look through the kitchen revealed nothing, except for some dirty dishes in the sink. Beside the sink was an old glass bong, it's burn cup charred black and sticky with res-inous residue. Gus went and looked in the bathroom. It was was filthy—the toilet bowl streaked and the grout between the tiles on the floor and walls of the shower stall were blackened with mold—but all Gus found was a few bottles of prescrip-tion pills on the edge of a tiny wall-mounted sink. The labels had been stripped off, so he couldn't tell what the bottles con-tained. Gus put them in an evidence bag he pulled from one of his pockets—he would send them off to the state crime lab for analysis.

Gus met Buzz back in the living room section of the trailer. Buzz had tossed the bedroom, which was already in a state of dishevelment, and looked through Jack's small closet. He came out of the bedroom holding a sandwich-sized baggie full of a greenish brown substance, that had been sitting on Jack's bedside table.

"This your weed, Jack?" Buzz called to the man outside.

"It's legal," Jack called back. "Less than an ounce. Private use. You guys are supposed to ignore it."

"Really?" Gus called back. "You an expert on the law now, Jack?"

There was silence from outside.

Together, Buzz and Gus removed the bulky cushions from the sofa, revealing a built-in plywood base underneath. But this one had an inner section cut out with an inset door hinged on one side. There was a rope pull for a handle. Gus pulled the door open and they both saw the mounting hooks inside, a rack not unlike those that hang in the back windows of hunters' pick-ups. Resting on one set of hooks was a black Armalite AR-15 rifle. It had no clip inserted so it was quite light when Gus lifted it out of the space underneath the sofa. He sniffed the barrel end of the rifle and caught the unmistakable odor of gunpowder. Gus looked at Buzz and nodded. "Bingo," he said.

Buzz came back out of the trailer first, carrying evidence bags containing the baggie of weed and the two pill bottles. Jack Ferro glanced up at him, saw what he had, and shook his head. Then Gus followed, holding the AR-15. Jack's head fell into his hands.

"I want a lawyer," he said, his voice small, muffled and defeated.

CHAPTER 13

Gus let Jack Ferro sit in one of the two small jail cells at the Little Penwick station for a couple of hours and think about things. They had let him put on his shoes and put him in the back of Buzz's Taurus. Then they drove around the Ferro property looking for a dark colored GMC SUV. They saw several pick-ups, but not the Acadia that they had seen in the CCTV camera scenes of the shooting.

It was late afternoon before Gus told Buzz to take the prisoner into the interview room. When he had been sitting in there for another thirty minutes, Gus nodded at his chief of detectives.

"OK," he said, "Let's do this."

"How do you want to play it?" Buzz asked. "You the bad cop, or is it me?"

Gus chuckled. "Don't think we're gonna need any of that," he said.

He was right. When the two officers walked in, closed the door and sat down, Jack Ferro, his face white and his eyes dancing back and forth between the two told them that he was frightened and ready to talk. Gus informed Jack that the interview was being recorded and read him his Miranda rights.

"Why'd you shoot up my police station?" was Gus' opening gambit. He could feel Buzz' intake of breath beside him.

"She told me to do it," he said, wringing his fingers together nervously. "That's her gun. She gave it to me. I've never owned a gun in my life. You can ask anybody. You can look up the records. I've never applied for a license. It's not mine. It's hers."

"You're talking about Janine Constance Stone," Gus said, looking down at the papers he held in his hand. "She gave you the gun and told you to shoot up the station?"

Jack nodded, vigorously. "Yep," he said.

Gus looked at him. "Why'd you do it, though?" he said. "I mean, even a dunderhead like you must know that it's not only illegal, it's dangerous to fire a weapon at a public building. Someone could have gotten hurt. Someone could have gotten killed. One of my officers sustained an injury. That's one count of assault on a law enforcement officer with a deadly weapon."

Gus turned and looked at Buzz sitting next to him. "What kinda rap does that get him?" he asked.

Buzz pursed his lips and cocked his head, thinking. "Usually that's a 20-year ticket," he said. "But of course, the judge will take the context into consideration. He could go up to 30. But he might take into consideration Jack's youthfulness and cut it all the way down to 15 years."

"Fifteen years?" Gus looked at Jack. "Well, hell, that's not so bad. You'll be out before you're forty."

Jack Ferro's eyes got big as he thought about that.

"So, why did you do it, Jack?" Gus said again, his voice softer this time.

Jack looked down at the metal table, then back up at Gus.

"She said I could avenge my family," he said. "You put Danny and Cosmo and Meels away. She said I had to do something for them."

Gus nodded thoughtfully. "Yeah, I get that," he said. "But of course, you'll be the one doing the time. Danny will probably get out long before you do. Might not have been the smartest thing in the world to do."

"Who was driving the truck?" Buzz jumped in with a question. His voice was hard-edged. It sounded like he wasn't kidding around. "We have you guys on camera. We've ID'd the truck. Who was driving it?"

Jack's face fell. "I can't tell you that," he said, his voice breaking. "Those guys will track me down and cut me up into pieces if I rat on 'em."

"We'll put you in jail for fifty years if you don't, punk," Buzz rasped. He pounded the table with his fist, making Jack jump back. "Who was the driver?"

"All I know is his first name," Jack said in a quavering voice. "He said to call him Manny. I don't know if that's his first name or his last. Or if it's really his name. He came and picked me up that morning. Janine left the gun in my place while I was at work. Then he drove into the station lot and stopped in front of the door and told me to blow the damn door down."

"So you did," Gus said, shaking his head. "Now you're in custody and this Manny fella is in the wind. Seems like you got the crap end of the deal, Jack."

Jack said nothing. He just shook his head back and forth slowly, eyes downcast. He was trying not to cry.

"I realize you did this because all your relatives are in jail," Gus said, "But there must be something else. Did she pay you?"

Jack cast his eyes down and didn't look either officer in the eye. "Yeah," he said, "She left two hundred bucks for me when she dropped off the gun. But she told me she'd get me another eight hundred once the job was done."

"And you trusted her?" Buzz couldn't keep the incredulity out of his voice.

"She's always been straight with me," Jack said. "She told me she's waiting to get some money, and once she did, she'd pay me the rest."

"Has she done that yet?" Gus asked.

Jack just shook his head. He was beginning to realize that he would probably never see the rest of the money. Or if he did, he would be in jail.

"I got another question for you, Jack," Gus said, rearranging his stack of papers. "Where is she?"

Jack looked up. "Who?" he asked. Then, realizing what a stupid question that was, he almost smiled. "Oh, you mean Janine?"

Gus didn't say anything, just looked at him across the table, steady, calm.

"I—I don't know ..." Jack began.

Buzz slammed his fist down on the table again. Jack jumped and flinched.

"Cut the crap, kid," he almost shouted. "Where is she?"

Jack wiped a hand across his forehead. "I don't know where she is right this second," he said.

"Where did you meet her?" Gus asked, his voice lower and calmer.

Jack shook his head. "I didn't," he said. "I mean, I didn't meet her in person. Only on the telephone. She called me about a week ago and told me what was going down. Told me I had to avenge the name of my family. Told me she'd get me the rifle, some guy would pick me up, and all I had to do was empty the magazine into the police station." He looked up at the two officers, pleading with them to understand. "It sounded like an easy grand," he said. "My truck needs some new tires."

"You talk to her a lot?" Gus asked. Buzz made a note in his notebook.

"Nah," Jack said, looking relieved. "I haven't seen her since the ring got busted up last year."

"You talk to her before last week?"

Jack shook his head. "Nope," he said. "I don't think any-one in the family has talked to her since Danny and them got arrested. She called me out of the blue."

"How'd you know it was her?" Gus asked.

Jack smiled, a secret knowledge kind of smile. "I knew her voice," he said. "We used to talk a lot, hang out, when she lived over at Dan's place. She's actually a pretty nice person. And, of course, she's kinda hot, too."

"So this voice from the past calls you up out of the blue, tells you you gotta go shoot up the local cop shop, and because your uncles and cousins and such got busted last year and sent away, you thought it would be just a great idea to do that? Is that what you're telling us?" Buzzy's angry, loud voice was like the edge of an executioner's axe, falling with a thud in the small, close room.

"Ah…yeah," Jack said. "That's what happened."

"Tell me more about this Manny dude," Gus said. "Who is he?"

Jack shook his head. "I dunno, man," he said. "I never saw him before in my life." He paused, thinking. "He's kinda fat, y'know? Big belly. Dark hair. Speaks pretty good for being, you know …"

"Hispanic?" Gus suggested. Jack nodded. "You said if you ratted him out, they'd come after you," Gus continued. "Who are we talking about? The mafia? The Russians? MS-13? Who would come for you?"

"I don't know," Jack said, sounding miserable. "One of those. Maybe all of them. Manny looked pretty evil, y'know? Like a tough guy. Tats on his neck and stuff. They looked like prison tats, y'know? Gang stuff. Not one you want to mess with."

Gus caught Buzz' eye and they got up and left Jack in the interview room. Gus led Buzz back to his office down the hall.

"Okay," he said, "We can book him. Three or four counts of assault. But how can we squeeze him? If she calls him back, I want to know about it."

Buzz stroked his chin as he looked up at the ceiling and thought.

"He'll probably make bail," he said. "Judge will put an ankle monitor on him. Maybe we can get authorization to tap his phone. Then, when the lovely Janine calls with the rest of his money, we'll be ready."

"That's assuming she calls," Gus said.

Buzz smiled. "What? You mean there is no honor among thieves?"

"Not usually, no," Gus said. "But let's try that route. Can you call the DA and set it all up?"

"Right-o," Buzz said and got up to go back to his office.

Jessica Martin stuck her head in Gus' doorway.

"Just got a call from New Bedford PD on the Acadia," she said. "They found an abandoned late model GMC. No plates, but they wonder if it's our vehicle. They've sent it over to forensics."

Gus nodded. "Good. Who is their chief detective over there?"

"Sofia Cortez," Jessica said. "She's top notch. Very thorough."

"OK. Call her back and ask if she knows any gangbanger over there goes by the name of Manny. Large fellow. Tats everywhere. Probably done time somewhere, hence the tats."

"Jackie give you this?"

Gus nodded. "This Manny fellow was the driver. Jack is afraid of him. Worried about him coming back on him."

"I'll tell Sofia to keep it on the low down," Jessica said, and went to make the call.

Gus sat back, feeling better than he had in a few days. They had found the shooters that had attacked the station, the car they did it in, and it was probably just a matter of time before the New Bedford PD picked up the driver. And he and Maggie seemed to be back on level ground again. That was a good thing. He knew they had a lot more things to talk about and decide, but they were at least communicating again. That was a relief.

He looked at his overflowing In box and glanced at the clock. It was almost six.

That crap can wait until morning, he thought.

CHAPTER 14

The next day, Jessica Martin drove to the Ferro compound deep in the swamp. She had called Catarina Ferro, Danny's wife, and asked to come over for a chat. Jessica drove a squad car and parked it outside the two-story white clapboard house with the wooden porch in front. Gus ordered Dottie Adams to dispatch one of the patrolmen on the day watch to join her at the Ferro place. It was something of an unwritten department rule that all visits to the Ferro place required at least one backup unit. With the long history between the Little Penwick Police Department and various members of the Ferro family, that rule made a lot of sense.

Jessica waited until Freddie Benes arrived before she got out of her car. She went over to Freddie's cruiser and told him she would probably be inside for a half hour, maybe a bit longer. If she didn't come back outside in an hour, he was to come looking for her.

She climbed the stairs to the porch and knocked on the front door. Catarina must have been watching and waiting, because the door opened almost immediately.

"Mrs. Ferro?" Jessica said, "I'm Lieutenant Jessica Martin."

"Come in, come in" said Catarina and stood back out of the way to let her enter. Danny Ferro's wife was probably in her mid-forties. Jessica knew that she and Danny had three kids, the oldest around seventeen. But this woman looked older. She was short and stout, with thick, heavy arms and legs, dark hair, dark eyes. She wore chino pants and a loose fitting top of some kind, but despite the billowy fabric, Jessica could see Catarina's pendulous breasts. The Ferro family was Portuguese, originally from the Cape Verde islands, and Catarina looked every inch of the Old World middle-aged housewife with several kids and a weight problem.

Catarina led Jessica into the living room, an open room in the front. The windows looked out on the porch and the street beyond. The furniture was fairly new and there was colorful artwork on the walls.

"Would you like some tea?" Catarina asked. Jessica could detect a slight foreign accent in the woman's voice. Her dark eyes were wary, her face frowning.

"That would be lovely, thanks," Jessica said. Catarina disappeared into the kitchen and Jessica, sitting in an upholstered wingback chair, looked around. There was a large flatscreen television dominating one corner of the room, and all the seating was arranged to face in that direction. There was an ornate and heavy looking cocktail table in front of the three-seat sofa and another chair matched the one Jessica occupied. There were two matching paintings showing an old village scene, with sun-bleached streets and buildings and an old donkey hauling two wicker baskets filled with freshly cut flowers. Opposite the television corner was a brick-faced fireplace. Shelves above the fireplace held some dark colored ceramic bottles and bowls and a wicker basket that looked handmade.

Catarina came back into the living room carrying a tray with cups and saucers, a teapot and silver dispensers for sugar and cream. The woman put the tray down in the cocktail table, sat down on the sofa and poured them each a cup.

"Thank you," Jessica said when she was handed her tea. They each sipped. Catarina put her cup down.

"So," she said, staring at Jessica, "What you want?"

"Have you been up to visit Danny?" Jessica asked. "How is he?"

Catarina raised her eyebrows. She wasn't expecting that question.

"Si," she said, "Yes. I have been to visit the prison where you put my husband. It is a long drive to Devens, north of Boston. It is difficult for me to go every weekend, like Danny wants. I have children to raise, and they come first. But I go when I can. He is my husband."

"I understand it can be difficult," Jessica said. "Is he doing okay in prison so far?"

Catarina rolled her eyes. "As well as he can," she said. "There are others like Danny in the jail there, and they watch out for each other. There are also some bad men there. It is very dangerous."

"Yes," Jessica said. "Jails can be dangerous. That's why it is better if you don't break the law, like Danny did."

Catarina was silent, but her eyes darted side to side. She wanted to say something, She probably wanted to scream something. But she maintained her composure and said nothing.

"I wanted to talk to you about somebody else today," Jessica said, sipping more of her tea. "I wanted to talk to you about Janine Stone."

"That *prostituta*," Catarina said, her voice a hiss. "She is the reason my husband is not here to raise his children."

"She lived here, in this house, did she not?" Jessica said.

"Yes," Catarina said. "My husband invited her to live here. He and his mother, Margarite, insisted she live in this house."

"You don't sound like you were happy about that arrangement."

Catarina shrugged. "It is my husband's home. It is my husband's wish," she said. "I am bound to do as he wishes."

"Were they sleeping together?"

The question brought Catarina to her feet. Jessica felt that she wanted to strike out at somebody at the thought of the idea. But instead, the woman walked over to the mantel and straightened the rectangular wicker basket there.

"No," Catarina said, her voice a bare whisper now. "My husband would never be unfaithful. It is against our religion to do such a thing. He would never do that."

"I see," Jessica said. "Have you talked with Janine Stone in recent months?" she asked. "Has she called here to talk with you?"

Catarina came back to the sofa from the fireplace and sat down again on the sofa. Her tea was untouched, steam rising slowly into the air.

"Yes," she said finally. "She called to me about a week ago."

"What did she say?" Jessica said. "What did she want to talk to you about?"

"She want to know if Danny say anything to me about money," Catarina said. "She think Danny has money belong to her. I tell her this is not true. He has nothing, Danny. He is in the jail. He try to stay alive so he can come home and be with his family again."

"So you don't know anything about any money that Danny might have been holding for Janine when she went away last fall?"

"No," Catarina said. "Of course not. There is no such thing." She stood up again and went to look out the front window. She could see Freddie Benes sitting in his police car at the end of the drive. There was not much else to look at.

"Are you sure?" Jessica pressed. "No boxes or crates Danny left behind? Nothing in the garage you have out back?"

From the window, Catarina was shaking her head, emphatically. "No," she said. "I know of nothing like that."

"Would you mind if I had an officer come over and look?" Jessica said. "Maybe he did leave something and did not tell you about it."

Catarina turned from the window and looked at Jessica with imploring eyes. "Why you do this to me?" she said, her voice wavering slightly. "Why you give me this trouble? I do nothing wrong. I do not break law. But here I am with my children to raise. Alone. How am I to do that? Why do you not care about that?"

"Catarina," Jessica said, keeping her voice soft and empathetic, "I do care about you. I am a mother, too, and I know how difficult it can be to raise children. I want to help you, not hassle you."

Catarina made a humph noise. She wasn't buying any of that. Especially from the police. Both in the Old World and here in Little Penwick, she had been trained to distrust the police. The police took. The police hurt. They did not help.

"If there is money that Danny left behind," Jessica continued, "If he did hide some money somewhere and you find it, the law says that you can keep that money. It's yours. You can use it for the children, for food, for clothes. If we find it, the police, we can keep the money under rules of civil forfeiture. If we find it, you won't get a dime. I don't want that. I'd rather you get to keep the money. But you have to help me find it."

Catarina was shaking her head again, slowly, back and forth.

"No," she said. "I know nothing about this money. I tell you what I tell that prostituta, that witch Janina … go away from me. It is not problema that belongs to me."

Jessica was planning her next argument when there was a knock on the door. Catarina went to answer it, and Jessica saw Freddie Benes standing on the porch.

"Yes, ma'am," he said when the door opened, "I'm just checking to see if my lieutenant needs anything."

Jessica glanced at her watch and saw that she had been talking with Catarina for just under an hour. She got up and went to the door.

"Thank you for your time, Catarina," she said to the woman. She handed her a business card. "If you think of anything else that would be helpful to us, please call me. And if you hear again from Janine Stone, understand that we are looking for her. If she contacts you again, please let us know immediately."

Catarina took the card but said nothing. When Jessica stepped out onto the porch, the door closed behind her. She heard the metallic sound of the lock being thrown.

CHAPTER 15

Don't let anyone *fool you. Tell you different. These people up here in Rhode Island are idiots. Morons. Lacking in intelligence. I mean, I come from Florida, where we know something about stupid people. We have loads of them ourselves. But we also have about twenty-one million people in Florida. Stands to reason a certain percentage of them are gonna turn out to be idiots.*

But Rhode Island has just about a million residents. I'd say half of them fall into the moron category. Maybe more.

So I called that Catarina bitch. Dumb as a fence post. Ugly, too. She came over from Santiago, just outside the capital of Praia, about twenty-five years ago, to marry Danny. It was an arranged marriage, just like they used to have like in the Middle Ages. Margie told me all about it. She was doing the negotiations for her grandson, Danny. Told me they had to pony up five thousand dollars to Catarina's family back in the islands. Dowry. Incredible, right?

Anyway, I called the bitch and demanded she tell me where Danny hid my money. She played dumb, said she didn't know anything about anything. Well, 'played dumb' isn't quite right

... she is dumb, so she wasn't playing. But she insisted she didn't know where he put my money. She's a liar and an idiot. She knows where it is.

So I called little Jack. That's what I always called him. He was about sixteen, seventeen when I came up here to live. Horny as a toad. You could almost always see he had a boner whenever I came into a room. Believe me, I know all about teen age boys.

Anyway, I knew I could talk little Jack into almost anything. I was right. I left two hundred bucks and a rifle in his trailer when he was out working. Ricardo gave me the name of this gangbanger from down in New Bedford. Manny somebody or other. He cost me another two hundred, just to drive the car. No questions. Hey, you know what they say ... Rhode Island is the 'I know a guy' state, right?

So little Jack pumped some rounds into Gus Haddock's building. I'll bet they were running around for days afterwards, wondering what the hell was going on. When I heard on the TV that shots had been fired down there, it was like I had just won the marathon or something. Fist pump! You go, girl!

Of course, I told Jack I'd get him more cash. I will. But I gotta find Danny's stash, first. I mean, my stash. I'm thinking there's at least half a million. We were going to buy another oil truck and let Danny do his thing on that one, too. I think Ricardo fronted Danny some cash for that, in addition to the usual payments that were coming down from Providence. Put it all together and it started to add up.

But I gotta find it. I got some ideas. I knew Danny pretty well. I knew how he thought. He could be a tricky little shit.

Smart, but tricky. So I'm looking. And when I find it, I'm out-ta here, toot sweet. Way too many idiots up here. I'm afraid the stupid will rub off on me. I can't let that happen. I got too many plans.

CHAPTER 16

Gus had a busy morning planned. He had invited four candidates to come down for an interview for the new job openings in the department. Two of the candidates were women, one was a black guy and the fourth was a white guy. As Gus was reviewing the application files on his desk, he thought to himself that the white guy had the most to prove, which wasn't really fair. The others might have some kind of issue in their backgrounds ... low GPAs in high school, or some kind of disciplinary event ... but those would be overlooked because of their race or gender. But not the white guy. He was already suspect just because he was the same color and sex of most of the police officers Little Penwick had ever hired. How crazy was that?

But all Gus could do was shake his head and deal with it. Reality sometimes comes up and smacks you in the head. This was what the culture demanded in this day and age. Gus was just trying to find the two best probational officers to join his department and, hopefully, to be effective as they served and protected the people of Little Penwick. When it came to crunch time, when a police officer was sorely needed, nobody would give a sweet damn what color or sex or nationality the officer was. They'd just want him or her to show up and arrest the bad guy, shoot the rabid dog, talk the cat down out of the tree or do CPR on someone having a heart attack.

Gus had scheduled the candidates to come in all on the same morning. He planned to spend thirty minutes with each of them, one right after the next. Power interviewing. Get it over with.

The first candidate showed up five minutes before nine. Jessica Martin was covering at the front desk, and she buzzed Gus.

"A Miss Williams is here for her appointment," she announced.

"Send her in," Gus replied.

Cassandra 'Cassie' Williams was tall with short dark hair and a bright smile. She was dressed in black slacks, a white T-shirt and a light gray coat. She came in brimming with confidence, shook Gus' hand with a firm handshake and perched on the edge of one of his guest chairs, folding her legs primly to one side. Her file said she was a recent graduate of the Rhode Island Municipal Police Training Academy at the community college in Lincoln, up in the north of the state. That meant she had basic training in police procedures, criminal law, firearms training, highway accident response, community patrolling, emergency services and was reasonably physically fit.

"So," Gus said, looking at the young woman over the top of her file, "Why do you want to work here in Little Penwick?"

"To tell you the truth, Chief Haddock," she replied, "I'm looking for my first job in law enforcement. It doesn't really matter if I work in Little Penwick or in Cranston or in Woonsocket. I need to get experience. Of course, I know about this town, and have been down here before. But to answer your question, I think starting out in a small town like this would be great. Give me the chance to get to know the citizens, one on one. Build relationships. They tell me that the most effective policing happens when people trust each other."

Gus nodded as she spoke. Obviously, she had been prepped for his question and she gave a pretty good answer. Whether she really believed what she was saying was another question. And probably one that could not be answered. At least, not sitting here in the chief's office.

"Any cops in your family?" he asked next.

Cassie smiled and shook her head. "I'll be the first one," she said. "My dad is a supervisor at a ball bearings factory over in Warwick. Mom stayed home and raised me and my two brothers."

"What do they think about you, wanting to be a cop?"

Her smile deepened. "Truthfully?" she said, "They think I'm crazy. Or that I've watched too many episodes of CSI or Hawaii 5-0." She paused, thinking. "Lotta people my age think the cops are bad, through and through. Racist ... bullies ... corrupt. Maybe they are, though I don't think most cops are like that. But the only way I can make policing better is to become one and do the job the right way. That's sorta my secret goal."

"Not a bad goal to have," Gus said. "What about your friends?"

"My good friends are fine with it," she said. "Some others dropped away when I enrolled in the police academy. Like my high school boyfriend. I think he thought I was going to arrest him for smoking weed or something."

"I can arrange to have him shot, if you'd like," Gus said. But he smiled when he said it.

She caught his smile and laughed. "He deserves that, but not just for dropping me," she said. "I was never that serious about Chuck. He was just my high school honey. But it was interesting to see how he reacted. A few others, too." She shook her head a little sadly. "Their loss, not mine."

Gus stood up. "Thanks for coming in, Cassie," he said, shaking her hand. "You've got a great record and a ton of potential. I'll be making my decision here in a week or two. I've got two positions open and, as you probably expect, quite a few good candidates. I'll be in touch."

She shook his hand again, with the same firm grip as before. "Thank you, Chief Haddock," she said. "I appreciate your time."

Gus had just enough time to get himself another cup of coffee from the break room when the next candidate was announced.

LaToya Crenshaw was also a recent grad of the RI-MPTA. Her grade point average was a bit lower than Cassie Williams' had been. She was a resident of Providence and a graduate of Classical High. She was short, just a bit over five feet, and round in shape. She wore a nice business suit, including the leather briefcase carried with a strap over her shoulder. When she came into Gus' office and perched on one of his guest chairs, she dropped the case to the ground at her feet.

"Welcome to Little Penwick," he said after shaking her hand. Her grip was softer and lighter than Cassie's had been. "You ever been down here?"

"I don't think so," LaToya said, shaking her head. "You got a 'hood down here?"

Gus chuckled. "Probably not the kind you're used to," he said. "Lots of rich people up in The Heights, lot of fishermen down by the harbor. Different hoods for different folks."

She smiled. "I guess that's right," she said.

She told Gus about her childhood in the hood she grew up in. Her father left home when she was a toddler. She had been raised by her mother and grandmother. School, church, home. Got decent grades in high school and was excited to be accepted at the police academy.

" Any cops in your family?" Gus asked.

"Yes," LaToya said. "I have an uncle on the force in Bridgeport and his son, my cousin, is in training in a small town near there. They're both good dudes."

"You think you can get used to the cultural differences, between here and Providence?" Gus asked.

"Never know 'til we try, I guess," LaToya said. "Crime is crime, wherever it happens."

"That's true," Gus nodded. "But policing in a town like Little Penwick isn't always about crime."

"It's not?"

"No," he said. "In fact, we probably go weeks, even months, without arresting anyone. Down here, there's a lot more service work, helping in the community. Don't get me wrong … our officers still patrol, look for signs of trouble, pull over drunk drivers, sometimes have to step in between a couple of drunks yelling at each other over the volume of the television set."

"Domestics," LaToya said, nodded as she followed what Gus was saying.

"That's right," he said. "We get a few of those. But not as many as they handle at the Providence PD, I'm guessing. What I'm getting at here is your expectation level. Do you think you'll be happy in a rural setting like we have here?"

"I think so," she said. "There ain't no milking cows or plucking no chickens, is there?"

Gus laughed. "There's actually a lot of that going on in this town, but not in my police force," he said. "You have any questions of me?"

"What's the starting pay?" she said.

Gus told her. He noticed her eyebrows went up slightly when she heard the starting salary.

" Another difference between Little Penwick and Providence," he said. "But rents are a bit cheaper down here."

Her eyebrows went up again. "I gotta live in the town to work here?" she asked. "I was gonna get my own crib up in the city."

"No," Gus said, "There's no requirement to live in the town. In fact, out of my staff of ten officers currently, I think one lives in Little Penwick. If you're willing to make the drive down here every day, I'm fine with it."

"Okay, then" she said, nodding to herself.

"Anything else?"

"Health insurance?"

Gus nodded. "Usual town plan," he said. "Blue Cross. Low deductible and co-pays. And a very good life insurance rider, in case you get shot while on the job."

"I ain't getting no shot," LaToya said. "You can keep that mess."

"I like your attitude," Gus said. He stood up. "Thanks for coming in. I've got a few more candidates to interview, then I'll be making my decision in a couple of weeks."

She shook his hand, soft, receding. Gus thought she didn't like the talk about getting shot on the job. What can I say, he thought, it's part of the job. Some can handle it, some can't.

Daniel Jackson was the next candidate to arrive. He had the body of a middle linebacker: barrel chest, no neck, arms and thighs like slabs of beef. Gus peeked at his file while he was sitting down and noticed he had indeed played football for Seekonk High in neighboring Massachusetts. His fuzzy hair was short and trimmed in sharp edges around the contour of his forehead and temples. He was dressed in a light gray suit with a blue dress shirt and nice patterned tie. He, too, carried a briefcase. Gus wondered if all the teachers at the police academies recommended their students carry one to all job interviews.

He shook Gus' hand with his own massive slab of a hand, and Gus was thankful his grip was firm but not knuckle-crushing. Daniel looked like he could crush anyone's hand without thinking twice about it.

Jackson had come from the Mass. Police academy north of Worcester. He had grown up across the Taunton River from Fall River, earning better than average grades in high school. His police academy transcripts showed that his professors — mostly retired cops — had liked his work ethic and his attitude. Gus saw that his marksmanship was especially strong. Gus knew that finding someone who was familiar and comfortable with guns was a challenge in this day and age. Points for Daniel, he thought.

"You work out a lot?" was his first question.

Daniel smiled. "Pretty regular, yeah," he said. "I had a real good coach up in Seekonk. Taught us the difference between just lifting weights, and lifting weights to accomplish something you wanted in your body. Came in real handy for the football team, but I liked how it made my body look and feel strong. So I keep it up."

"We're a pretty small town," Gus said. "Not nearly as much action as Fall River or Taunton or Providence. That a problem?"

"Nossir," Jackson answered. "I'm interested in all aspects of police work. Community service. Working with kids. Helping old folks find the right social services." He paused, thinking. "Of course, I imagine Little Penwick has its own set of problems. Property cases. Traffic control. Maybe some drunk driving." He held up a finger and bent over, opening and then fishing through his briefcase. He found what he was looking for and sat up, holding a sheaf of papers.

"   According to the state crime reports — the latest figures I have are from last year — Little Penwick saw a twenty-two percent increase in DUI cases last year. And that was after a twelve percent increase the year before. But the good news is that burglaries were down seven percent."

"Does that show how many burglary cases, total, there were last year?" Gus asked.

Daniel studied his papers. "I don't think so," he said. "No… wait! Here it is. There were … three." He looked again. "Is that right?" he said. "That sounds really low."

"That's about right," Gus said. "Our year-round population in Little Penwick is just under five thousand. In the summer, that can double and even a little more."

"Wow," Daniel said, looking across the desk. "That's not a lot of people."

Gus shrugged. "Smaller town," he said. "Smaller crime rates. Crime is a direct proportion of population. You got a city with five million people, you're gonna get lots of crime, of all kinds. Five thousand? They'll call the department if a chicken gets out of the coop."

Daniel laughed. "Well, I guess I'd better be prepared to arrest some chickens, then," he said.

They talked for a few more minutes, before Gus ended the interview with his usual spiel and got ready for the last candidate.

Bill Dawson was tall and tanned, with sun-bleached blond hair, and Foster Grant sunglasses parked atop his head. He wore chino slacks, a white oxford shirt, no tie, loafers with no socks. He didn't have a leather briefcase, but he did walk in with a wide, friendly smile.

"Howdy, there, Chief," he said as he came into Gus' office and took a guest chair. "Man, I can't believe how deep in the sticks it is down here. I counted six farms coming down Main Street. Lost track of how many cows. Real pretty country, tho."

"Road," Gus said.

"Howszat?"

"It's Main Road, not Main Street," Gus said. "Small difference, but important to know."

"Right," Bill said. "Main Road. Got it."

Dawson said he had grown up in East Greenwich, a fairly affluent town on the West Bay. He had graduated from East Greenwich High, then attended the University of Rhode Island for four years, majoring in criminal justice.

"Do you know Charles Rahel?" Bill asked.

Gus looked at him. "Can't say that I do," he said.

"Well, he's my cousin," Bill said. "Second cousin, actually, if you're keeping track. Anyway, he's in the state legislature. Sits on the Criminal Justice committee. He's got connections, if you know what I mean."

Gus nodded.

"And I've got some letters of recommendation I can send you," Bill continued. "Vinny Manning was the head Colonel of the State Police. He just left to be the town manager out in Exeter. But he wrote me a good recommendation letter. And the chief of the East Greenwich department also wrote me a nice letter. I'll send those down here to you. You have e-mail, right?"

"Right," Gus said. "We do."

"Excellent," Bill said, looking pleased with himself.

"Do you happen to know the attorney general?" Gus asked. "Preston Knox?"

"The AG?" Bill looked perplexed. But just for a few moments. "I don't think I've ever met him in person," he said. "But I think my Dad said he's seen him around the country club from time to time. I'm sure I can get to meet him, have him write something up for me. Would that help?"

"Could not possibly hurt," Gus said.

"Righteous," Bill said. "I'm on it."

"You got any questions for me?" Gus asked.

"When do I start?" Bill said. "Reason I ask is because we're planning a trip down to Bermuda in August. There's a killer sailing regatta down there and Dad needs me to crew for him. You ever been to Bermuda? Dark n' Stormies, my man. But you gotta watch it, they'll sneak up on you and kick your ass."

Gus looked at the kid for a moment. "That shouldn't present a problem," he said finally. "I'm sure we can find a way to work around your schedule. And thanks for the advice on the cocktails. I'll try to stay out of their way."

Bill nodded happily. "Beautiful," he said. "Anything else you need?"

"I believe I am, as your crowd likes to say, cool," Gus said. "Thanks for coming in."

"You betcha," Bill said, shook Gus' hand and pranced out of his office.

"Righteous," Gus said, mostly to himself, as the young man left.

Jessica Martin strolled in after Dawson left. "So," she said, smiling at Gus. "How'd that go? Find anybody good?"

"Three out of four," Gus said. "That'd make me an All Star if I was batting for the Sox."

"But we only have two positions open," Martin said. "You'll have decide which one to eliminate."

"Oh, yeah," Gus said. "That must be why this town pays me the big bucks."

"I'm sure it is," she said.

CHAPTER 17

THE NEXT MORNING, Gus was working away at the paperwork on his desk. Freddie Nunes at the front desk buzzed his phone.

"Chief," he said, "You've got a call."

"Who is it?"

"Well, he says his name is Slate Evans," Freddie said. "Same name as that rock star on The Slayers. Might be a hoax call, but he does have an accent."

"I'll take, it, Freddie, thanks," Gus said.

He picked up his phone. "Chief Haddock," he said.

"Chief?" said the voice on the phone. "Thank goodness you're in. I'm going slow motion bonkers over here."

"That you, Slate?" Gus said.

"Yeah, yeah," Evans said. "I really need your help, mate."

"What can I do for you?"

"I need to get out of the house," he said. "Been here for five days. Place is crawling with people I don't know, didn't invite. I gotta get outta here, get some fresh air."

"You got a car?" Gus said.

"Yeah, mate, 'course I do."

"You got a driver's license?"

There was a pause.

"I'm serious, mate," he said. "You have no idea what this place is like. I think every record producer on the East coast is sleeping in my bedrooms, eatin' all me bloody food. Can't think, can't play my axe. I'm up the rope, lad."

"Sounds awful," Gus said. "Why don't you tell everyone to go home?"

There was another pause.

"I can't do that, mate," he said. "Long story, but the record company actually owns part of this place. I can't give 'em the heave-ho."

"Bad luck," Gus said. "What do you want me to do?"

"Get me out of here," Evans said. "Take me someplace in Little Penwick where I can sit and think for an hour or two."

"I'm the chief of police," Gus said. "I can arrest someone, or shoot them. Those are about the only two choices."

"Naw, mate," he said, "Too medieval. Listen, can I buy you lunch? If you'll come pick me up, I'll buy. I gotta get out of this place or something bad is going to happen."

Gus glanced at his watch. It was eleven thirty.

"OK," he said, "I'll be over in fifteen minutes."

"Ta, chief," Evans said. "You're a bloody lifesaver."

Gus pulled his squad car to a stop next to the elaborate brick-and-wrought iron gate outside the Evans mansion. He waited for a minute. A figure dressed in jeans, a black cape and a 1940s-style fedora came out of the gate and jumped in the front seat.

"Go, go go!" Slate Evans said. "I think King is on to me!"

Gus pulled away. Evans looked back over his shoulder to see if anyone was following.

"Nice cape," Gus said as he drove down Cabot Reef Road. "You the bat man?"

Evans smiled. "I've been told it's dashing," he said. "And I needed a disguise to get away from my security dudes."

"Like they've never seen a rock star wearing crazy-ass stuff before," Gus said. "Aren't they supposed to, you know, guard and protect you and stuff?"

"Tell you the truth, I don't know what they're supposed to do," Evans said. "They're not my security, they belong to the record company. So I don't trust them as far as I can throw 'em."

Gus said nothing, but continued to drive.

"Where are we going?" Evans said. "Hope it's no place in public."

"I thought you were going to buy me lunch," Gus said. "Lunch usually takes place in a restaurant, which often has people also eating there. They call those people 'the public.'"

Evans looked at Gus. "You've never been an international rock star, have ya, gov?' he said.

Gus laughed. "Not so far," he said.

Evans shook his head. "Well, when you are, you will discover that you can't go out in public anymore. No restaurants. No movies. No shops. Feckin' people'll come crowding in, asking for autographs or just to talk about their favorite Slayers song, or whatever. And that's just the guys. The ladies are bloody vicious. Bloody impossible, it is."

Gus continued to drive. He was heading toward Crescent Beach.

"I know a place," he said. "People will mostly leave you be."

"We'll see," Evans said, sounding dubious. "But thanks, mate. Appreciate it."

Gus nodded and continued driving. In a few minutes, he turned onto a dirt road next to a large maple tree and drove down past a swamp until the drive came out in the opening in front of the Star Rider's clubhouse. There were five bikes lined up outside the front door.

"A motorcycle club?" Evans said, reading the sign above the door. "Like the Hell's Angels? You tryin' to get me killed?"

"Naw," Gus said. "I'm told the food is good here. And the patrons are all probably big fans of The Slayers. And have been since the Sixties."

Gus held the door as Evans walked through. Inside, the one big room was cool, painted all in white. Somewhere, an air conditioner was pumping cool air through the vents. There were some black leather sofas and chairs on one side, and a group of six or seven tables on the other. The seating group was empty, but three of the tables were full of people eating lunch. On the back wall, there was a rectangular pass-through window above a counter, and through the window, Gus could see the Big O, Ernie O'Connell, preparing some sandwiches in the kitchen. O'Connell put the plate on the counter and rang the little bell. "Order up!" he called. Someone from one of the tables got up and collected his lunch.

O'Connell looked through the window and saw Gus and immediately came out of the kitchen through the swinging door next to the pass-through counter, wiping his hands on his apron.

"Chief Haddock!" he said, "Welcome back to the Riders."

They shook hands. Gus turned to introduce Evans, but immediately noticed that introductions were not required.

"Jay-sus Christy," O'Connell said, staring at Evans' crevassed face. "Of all the gin joints in the world, you walk into mine."

"Hullo, mate," Evans said. "I'm …"

"I know who you are," Ernie said. "And you are most welcome. When I was in Nam in '69, we practically wore out your record, Overthrow. I memorized your solo on air guitar."

"Riiiight," Slate said, looking a little befuddled.

Gus broke in, as O'Connell was staring at Evans as if he was a teen-age boy and Scarlett Johansson has just walked in. "Ernie, Slate here wanted some lunch, but didn't want to face gobs of people. I thought we could wrangle him up a nice quiet lunch here. Maybe a beer or two."

"You want me to get rid of this trash?" O'Connell said, nodding over his shoulder at the other people having lunch at the tables. "Just say the word and they're gone."

"Not necessary, my man," Evans said, patting O'Connell on the shoulder. "In fact, please give me all of their lunch tickets. I'll pay for the lot." He reached into his pocket and pulled out a wad of bills. He counted out four hundred dollar bills and handed them over to the Big O.

"That's very kind of you," the Big O said, pocketing the cash and ushering Evans and Gus to an open table. "Please, come sit down. What kind of beer you like? Got some Guinness. Got some Mexican. Got some local stuff, though I can't really recommend it. Kinda hoppy for my taste."

Gus and Slate sat down. "Bring us a couple of stouts," Gus said. O'Connell nodded, then turned and addressed the other diners.

"Listen folks," he said, "We got a guest in the club here today. Won't tell you who, but I'm sure you can figure it out. But there's two things you need to know. One, our guest here has picked up your lunch, out of the goodness of his heart. Two, he wants a nice, quiet lunch. So if you want to ever come back to the Star Riders Motorcycle Club, you will do what he wants and leave him alone. You got that?"

He glared at the other diners. Who all stared at Slate Evans as if the Saviour himself had walked into the place.

"And Chief Haddock here has my permission to shoot anyone who approaches the table," O'Connell said. He gave a final, venomous look. "As you were."

The other diners bent their heads down and continued eating, with only an occasional peek over to the table where Slate Evans took off his hat and sat down with Gus, the Big O hovering next to them.

"The special today is hot pastrami," O'Connell said. "On toasted rye, with Swiss cheese and spicy mustard. Sides of fries and slaw."

"Love a good pastrami," Evans said, with a grin. "You, too, chief?"

Gus nodded and the Big O went back into the kitchen. He came back out with two flagons of dark beer, then retreated once again.

"So," Gus said when they were alone. "Why am I really here?"

Slate looked at him, eyebrows raised, a wry smile on his face. "You didn't buy the 'I need to get outta here' thing?"

"Not really," Gus said. "Somebody like you can get a limo, call a helicopter, order an ocean liner … any and all in about fifteen seconds flat. So, no, I'm not buying the need to escape thing. But I figure you did need me to talk about something. So, shoot."

Evans took a sip of his beer, looking appraisingly at Gus over the rim of his glass.

"I imagine people underestimate you all the time, mate," he said. "Bein' a small town copper with a good noggin. But you're right. I need some advice. From someone with experience with untrustworthy types. I'm up a rope and dunno which way to turn."

Gus drank a bit of his beer, savoring the almost caramel-like flavor, with the distinctive Guinness bite at the end.

"Best thing to come out of Ireland since U2," Gus said, smacking his lips a little.

"Don't forget Van the Man," Slate said, smiling. "He's a lovely man, Van is."

Gus smiled but kept silent. He figured Slate was going to tell him what he wanted sooner or later.

Slate let the silence last for a few seconds. He looked like he was thinking. Then he leaned forward, arms on the table.

"Look, mate," he said finally. "I'm just a guitar player, y'know? Grew up along the docks of East London. Never had two pence to rub together, yeah?" He saw something in Gus' eyes and tried to head it off. "I know, I know," he said, "Everyone thinks I'm this big international rock star ... oooh, he's one of the Slayers! ... and can do whatever the blazes I wanna do, yeah?"

Gus nodded. "Everybody thinks that because it appears to be so," he said.

"That's what I'm saying, mate," Evans said. "Looks is deceiving. I mean, I'm not saying that we've haven't all done well, because we have. Especially Jocko. He went off on his solo thing back in the Nineties and the rest of us in the band played gigs with friends and all until Jock finished doing some movies and decided it was time to get back to rockin'."

Gus nodded. He had just been a kid in the Nineties, but remembered when The Slayers went on hiatus so that Jock Morgan, the Slayers' flamboyant lead singer and sex symbol to millions, could pursue a solo singing career and film some movies in which he had played the lead.

"When we got back together, there was new management," Slate said. "Somewhere along the line, our old management agency had sold our backlist for about fifty million. Nice chunk of change for everyone, but we needed to refill the coffers when we started up again. So the record label, BMX, had us sign a new contract which gave them a lot of control, not only of our music, but our lives, too."

"Is that when they told Jock he had to divorce that starlet he was married to ... what was her name?"

"Meena Crosby," Slate said, with a grimace. "Christ, what an evil bitch that one was. And Jocko has taken up with quite a few losers over the years. But Meena? Sheer poison. So they told him she had to go or no deal."

"And she went," Gus said, sipping some more beer.

Slate nodded. "Then, while they were booking The Slayers in huge stadiums all over the world, the band got put on a salary."

"No shit?" Gus said, eyebrows raised, "Like fifty grand a year, plus perks?"

Slate nodded. "Bit more than fifty K, but yeah. We no longer owned the music or a piece of the brand," he said. "Imagine that. We created the brand of The Slayers by being The Slayers, and then they told us we couldn't get paid by the brand that we created! Feckin' ridiculous, right?"

"Sounds like something a bunch of lawyers would cook up," Gus said.

Slate pointed a long bony finger at Gus. "Damn right!" he said. "First kill all the feckin' lawyers."

Ernie O'Connell came out of the kitchen with a tray holding two plates, each with a sandwich and the sides. He put down the plates and went back into the kitchen. He was apparently obeying his own orders not to talk to Slate Evans.

"So what you're telling me is that The Slayers is now a corporation, owned by investors or some other faceless players, and you and the band just get paid an agreed-on set amount, no matter how much income you generate," Gus said.

"Spot on," Slate said. "But it's worse than that. They have control. They tell us where to play, when to play and, pretty much, what to play. We've written some killer new tunes in the last five years, and the management won't let us record and sell them. They tell us it will dilute the Slayers' brand if we bring out new music that's better than the old stuff. Some feckin' MBA looks at a spreadsheet and decides he knows better than us what our fans want. Can you even imagine?"

"Nope," Gus said. He couldn't imagine that one of the world's most famous group of rock musicians couldn't record the music they wrote and wanted to sing. "Have you and the band thought about getting a new lawyer and taking these guys to court?"

"'Course," Slate nodded. "But they thought of that and put a clause in our new contract. If we —any of us together or as individuals — hire an outside counsel, we can get sued, fired, have to pay back royalties … the whole lot. Got us by the short 'n' curlies, they do."

Gus had been eating his sandwich while Slate was talking. It was pretty good. The pastrami was well-spiced and not too greasy. And it went well with his Guinness. Which was almost gone. He wondered if he should have another. After all, he was still on duty. He wiped his hands clean on a napkin.

"Well, that is interesting and all," Gus said. "But again … what do you want from me? I haven't heard anything yet that sounds like the law has been broken, so I guess you want me to go shoot a couple of those pesky lawyers?"

Evans had taken a huge bite out of his sandwich, and was trying to chew and swallow as fast as he could. When he was able to answer, he did.

"Yeah," he said, "I'd love that. And so would me mates in the band. But no, I have a more immediate problem."

Gus ate some more sandwich and waited. The Big O came out of the kitchen and looked at Gus, who nodded. O'Connell went back and came out with two more beers. Gus smiled his thanks.

"I just found out, yesterday or the day before, that I'm to host a big party for the Fourth of July," Evans said. "My mates on the Slayers are on hols all over the world, so they're not coming, but I'm told I'm expected to play with some other chaps that the record company will arrange. I don't get to decide if I want to do this … I'm being told I have to do it."

Gus said nothing, but just sipped his beer and looked at Slate. He still hadn't heard anything that he could take action on.

"So I got the list of the guys coming to play and did a little background checking," Evans said. He finished his sandwich and polished off the first glass of beer before reaching for the second.

"And?"

"And all the people they've booked to come down and play with me on the Fourth are local dudes," Evans said. "All under contract with one company, based in Providence."

"And that company is?" Gus was interested now.

"Something called Narragansett Talent," Evans said. "The CEO is some local guy. Italian fella. Named Giancarlo. Never heard of him before."

"Ricardo Giancarlo?" Gus said, sitting up a little straighter.

"That's the one," Evans nodded. "You know him?"

"I've crossed paths with him from time to time," Gus said. "He is associated with a group of gentlemen that often attract the attention of people like me."

"Ahh," Evans said, his dark eyes suddenly alight with excitement. "He's a bloody Godfather, innit? Bam. Bam. Leave the gun. Take the cannoli."

Gus chuckled. "Not quite that dramatic," he said. "He's more into leaving the gun and taking the money."

"Yeah, I get it," Evans said. "I mean, I'm already chuffed that they're making me do this big concert thing at my own house. But I'm also chuffed that they're telling me who I can play with and what songs we're gonna play."

"What happens if you don't?" Gus said. "Call a cab and have them take you to New York or something. What can they do if you don't do what they want?"

Evans looked at Gus. "I've been told it would not be in my best interests."

"You know what that means?" Gus asked.

Evans shook his head. "Nope," he said. "And I'm pretty sure I don't want to find out."

Gus glanced at his watch. "Well, it's been about an hour and you've finally told me something that sounds illegal," he said. "Pretty sure you can't be forced into doing something — in this case a performance — that you don't want to do. Even if you have a contract of some kind. And from what you've told me, you and your band have a contract with this record company, BMX, not with the locals up in Providence."

"Yeah, yeah, tell me more," Slate said, eyes gleaming.

"Now, BMX may well have a connection with Narragansett Talent," Gus continued. "Maybe they've invested money, maybe they have a joint marketing agreement. Whatever. I don't think Narragansett can legally force you to comply with your BMX contract, or try to enforce that contract as if it were their own."

"So I can tell them to jump?" Evans said.

"Sounds like it to me," Gus said. "But I am not a lawyer, I'm a cop. You should talk to someone with a law degree. You got a personal lawyer of some kind?"

"Yeah," Evans said. "My guy's over in Connecticut. I'll give him a call."

"Good plan," Gus said. He peeked at his watch again. "I need to get back to work …"

"Yeah, sure, I get it, mate," Slate said. "I appreciate you listening to me tales o' woe. And for finding me an excellent sandwich."

"There might be something I can do on this end," Gus said, staring at his beer.

"Yeah?"

"About that concert," Gus said. "Town has ordinances on public performances, ordinances on making too much noise after dark. Did this record company up in Providence say anything about obtaining a permit for the concert?"

"Don't think so," Evans said. "Can you close them down? I'd be very grateful."

Gus nodded. "Let me think on this for a day or two," he said. "I'll let you know."

Slate rose from the table. He turned and walked over to the other tables, where none of those who had been eating lunch when he and Gus walked in had left. He spent the next five minutes wandering from table to table, shaking hands, telling jokes, posing for photos and signing autographs. When he was done, he glanced at Gus and they walked out together.

"Good people," Slate said as they got back in the police cruiser. "Real. Honest."

"That's how we grow 'em down here," Gus said.

CHAPTER 18

AFTER HE GOT back from lunch with Slate Evans, Gus put in a couple of hours attacking the growing pile of paperwork on his desk. He went into Buzz Franklin's office for an update.

"Chief?" Dottie from dispatch poked her head in the door of Buzz's office. "You got a call. From Providence police department."

"Thanks Dot," Gus said. "I'll take it in my office."

When he picked up the phone, he couldn't hear anyone, just the noise of the phone being held tightly in the palm of someone's hand. He could hear muffled voices in the background. Finally, someone spoke.

"Hello? Chief Haddock? Is that you?"

"Gus Haddock here," Gus said.

"Chief, this is Dave Andrade, Providence PD," the voice on the phone said. "I don't think you and I have ever met, but I know your Dad pretty well. In fact, I used to work down there with him, years ago. Anyway, I'm the lieutenant with the Special Crimes Unit and we got a situation at the Sunrise Center over in Olneyville. I understand the director there, Maggie Wells, is, um, known to you ..."

"We're engaged," Gus said shortly. "Is it DeShawn? He come back for his woman?"

"He has," Andrade said. "This time he brought a heater. Has the place in a hostage situation."

"Is Maggie OK?" Gus felt his throat tightening and his ears began pounding.

"Everyone's fine, so far," Andrade said. "A little scared, but he hasn't shot anyone yet. Our hostage negotiation team is on the scene and talking with him."

"What's he want?"

Andrade chuckled softly. "Right now, he wants a pizza with everything on it. His woman isn't at the center, but he's demanding we bring her there or he said he's gonna start shooting some of the other, er, *bitches* in the place." He paused. "His word, not mine," he said.

"You gonna stall him for a while?"

"Oh, sure," Andrade said. "Standard procedure. Delay, delay, delay until he starts getting antsy. That's when he'll make a mistake and we can get the drop on him."

"Okay," Gus said. "I'm on my way. Tell whoever's in charge I'll be up there inside of an hour."

Gus found Jessica Martin in Buzz Franklin's office, going over some evidence on a breaking and entering case at a local seed and feed store. She smiled at him as he entered.

"Harvey Jenkins said someone broke a window in his store, crawled inside and stole five packets of zinnia seeds," she started to say. "Buzz and I are calling it the Great Zinnia Caper and ..." Then she looked at him. "What's wrong?"

"Some punk ass has Maggie and her clients in a hostage situation up in Providence," Gus said. "I'm going up to see what I can do."

"You want someone to go with you?" she asked.

"No," Gus said. "Just hold down the fort. I'll be back … when I'm done."

He ran out of the station, jumped in his marked SUV, hit the lights and the siren and blasted out of the parking lot, heading for Providence. In good times, when there was no weather and it wasn't rush hour, one could make the drive from Little Penwick to downtown Providence in about fifty minutes. With his siren clearing the way in front of him, it still took him ten minutes to make it up the two-lane Main Road to Route 24 in Tiverton, another five minutes at about 80 mph to the intersection with Interstate 195 in Fall River and then fifteen minutes straight on to Providence, at speeds well above 90.

He tried to concentrate on his driving, so he wouldn't go flying off the road. Besides, that helped him not to think about the situation at the Sunrise Center. He imagined that Maggie and her clients and staff were probably traumatized. He hoped that DeShawn understood that he'd get extra time in jail if he physically harmed any of the women at the center. He trusted that Maggie would keep a cool head. She normally did. But of course, now she was pregnant and her body was awash in all kinds of new and different hormones. He hoped she would remember that and try to keep a lid on it. He pressed the accelerator down a little further and blew past a grocery store semi truck like it was standing still.

His progress slowed when he hit the city. Apparently, people in Providence are so used to sirens and police vehicles that they rarely if ever move out of the way. Still. Gus made it over to Olneyville in minutes. As he approached the storefront location of the Sunrise Center, he saw the half dozen police vehicles parked at odd angles on the street and sidewalk outside the center, lights flashing. A crowd of onlookers had gathered across the street from the center.

He leaped out of his car and strode towards the front door of the center. A big and burly patrolman stepped in front of him, hands up. Gus flashed his badge. The patrolman pointed him to a group of officers and plainclothes men standing around the hood of one of the Providence PD cars on the street nearby.

"Gus Haddock, Little Penwick PD," he announced to them. "My finance, Maggie Wells, is the director of the Sunrise Center. What's the sitrep?"

"Chief Haddock," one of the plainclothes guys said, "I'm Deputy Chief Armand Lopez. Ms. Wells is fine, everyone inside is fine, so far. We've ordered a pizza for DeShawn Taylor which will buy us some time. He said he's hungry."

"You bringing his girlfriend over?"

Lopez cast a glance over at the other officers in the braintrust standing around the car. "We're talking about that right now," he said. "Some say we should bring her over. Might help defuse the situation. Others aren't so sure."

"I don't think I would," Gus said. "DeShawn knows he's going down for this. He probably blames Angelique for all his problems. Once he sees her, he might unload his clip into her, and maybe some of the others in there, just for fun. He's getting close to the nothing left to lose place."

Lt. Lopez nodded. "I feel the same way," he said. "We're playing out the string as long as we can. I expect he'll be asking for a getaway car pretty soon. We'll agree to that, but take a couple hours before we tell him it's coming. Longer this goes on, the better. The more time he has to think about this, about what he's done, the better the chance he'll decide to give it up."

"You got the back door covered?"

"Of course," Lopez smiled. "This ain't our first rodeo, Chief," he said.

"Anyway can I get in that way?" Gus said. "Maybe when he's occupied with his pizza. I could get a drop on him, put him down."

"If anyone's gonna do some cowboy shit, it's gonna be one of our own," Lopez said. "Why don't you come over and meet the group. You'll see. They're all good men. They know what they're doing."

"Yeah," Gus said. "OK."

Lopez turned to walk the twenty feet back to the front of the squad car where there were papers scattered across the hood. Probably floor plan layouts and maybe DeShawn's rap sheet. A half dozen men stood around, talking to each other and looking at the papers. None of them looked panicked. None of them looked mildly excited. Just another day, another hostage situation in good old Providence. Gus saw a delivery guy from Domino's walking down the sidewalk toward the center's front door, carrying a large box and looking at the street numbers to find the right one.

With Lopez' back turned, Gus moved quickly. He was ten steps from the front door. He covered that distance in two large bounds, grabbed the pizza box from the delivery guy, pushed on the door and stepped inside. Behind him, he heard a faint "Hey!" in protest.

The foyer inside the door was dark. Arthur Manville, the center's somewhat elderly security guard, was sitting in his folding chair, holding his head in his hands and moaning in pain. Obviously, he had been clocked by DeShawn. At least he hadn't been shot, Gus thought.

Turning to his left, he saw the long front room. As before, several women, Gus figured about ten, were sitting around on the couches and chairs. They all looked scared, and stared up at Gus with wide eyes. DeShawn was standing against the far wall, where he could keep an eye on everybody. Maggie was sitting in the middle of the couch, holding the hands of the women on either side of her.

"Pizza's here, DeShawn," Gus said loudly as he walked into the room. "Where do you want it?"

"Put it down on the table, Jack," DeShawn said, motioning at the cocktail table in front of the long sofa where the women were sitting. He pointed with the gun he held in his right hand. Gus got a quick look at it. It looked like a Smith & Wesson 9 mm. The gun had a short barrel, just about three inches, Gus figured. Harder to grab out of his hand. "And where is my Angelique? They said they was goin' to get her ass over here."

Gus bent over to put the pizza box down on the table and stood upright again.

"Dunno," he said, putting his hands out wide. "I'm just the delivery guy. I can go ask…"

He watched DeShawn's eyes. They looked red and slightly out of focus. Gus figured he was on something. Crystal, maybe. Hit of cocaine. Maybe one laced with fentanyl. Gus hoped not. That would make DeShawn even more lethal. As he watched, he saw the eyes swim back into focus and DeShawn did a double take.

"Hey," DeShawn said. "You that motherfucker copper what cracked my haid befo." He pushed himself off the wall and began to bring his gun hand up. Gus was about six feet away and faster than DeShawn's drug addled reactions. He threw himself at DeShawn, grabbing the gun hand and pushing it up, so the gun was pointed at the ceiling. DeShawn managed to squeeze off one round before Gus overpowered him. The sound of the report made everyone in the room jump and Gus heard a couple of the women scream in fear. With his left hand holding the gun, Gus swung his right elbow down and chopped DeShawn in the front of his throat. The blow was almost instantly disabling and DeShawn began making gagging noises and his gun-free hand came up and began scratching desperately at his throat. Gus yanked the little 9mm away and tossed it across the room. He pushed the helpless attacker down on the floor and put a knee into the back of his neck to keep him there.

Behind him, he heard Maggie quickly order the women in the room to flee. "Go…go!" she yelled, "Get out, get out now!" Almost simultaneously, the front door crashed open and three fully outfitted SWAT officers poured inside, their rifles sweeping back and forth across the room.

"I got him," Gus called out loudly. "It's over."

OF COURSE, IT wasn't over. After DeShawn was pulled up, handcuffed and led away to jail, Deputy Chief Lopez came up to Gus, face to face. Lopez was hot. "I don't know what kind of freak show you run down in Little Penwick, Haddock," he said, his face so close to Gus that he could smell what he had for lunch, "But up here, we have procedures and rules we follow. There could have been ten or a dozen women shot to death because of your cowboy act. I don't think I've seen such a complete clown show since the circus was last in town. Goddam it, Haddock, I'm going to ..."

Gus abruptly turned away from Lopez and went to find Maggie, who was standing outside, hugging two of the women who had been inside with her. He waited until they finished their teary group hug, and then he swept her into his arms.

"You OK?" he asked. She tightened her arms around him, but was silent. "I'll take that as a yes," he said. She hugged him tighter.

CHAPTER 19

Sᴇᴠᴇʀᴀʟ ʜᴏᴜʀꜱ ʟᴀᴛᴇʀ, Gus and Maggie were sitting in her loft condo. Gus had a cold beer. Maggie had poured herself a glass of white wine. Gus looked at her while she was doing that, but she had glanced at him and he very clearly read the mood on her face. *I'm drinking this and I don't give a crap what anyone says.* So he said nothing.

They sat down on her stylish sofa and looked out the bank of windows that framed the buildings of downtown Providence, gleaming gold in the late afternoon son. Neither one of them said anything for a while, but just sipped at their drinks and looked out the window. It was quiet, save for the noises that crept in from the city outside: traffic humming past on I-95 and some sirens in the distance.

Maggie leaned forward, put her wine glass down, then turned to look at Gus.

That's when she lost it. Her lips quivered, her eyes filled and then she burst into tears. He drew her into his arms.

"Let it out," he said. "Let it all out."

She cried for a good ten minutes, soaking his shirt with spots. He replayed the scene from the afternoon. After De-

Shawn had been taken away, Deput Chief Lopez went back to his office to continue his important work of supervising the grunts out on the street. Maggie had continued to move among her clients, hugging them and assuring them that they would be safe at the Center, now that DeShawn was gone.

Gus had chatted with the Providence cops remaining at the scene. There were still a few detectives left asking questions and measuring out distances inside the Sunrise Center for their reports. But the rank and file officers, one or two at a time, sauntered over to shake Gus' hand and congratulate him for the bold action that had stopped the hostage situation in its tracks.

"Bold move, bro," one of them had said to Gus. "They tell us up here not to do stuff like that. Could get the department sued if anyone gets hurt."

"What about stopping crime?" Gus had said. "That not important in Providence anymore?"

The cop had shrugged and smiled. "You met Chief Lopez, right?"

Gus understood. Didn't like it, but he understood.

Eventually, Maggie's sobs lessened and she sat up. Gus knew it was important for her to work her emotions out, empty the jug, think of all the terrible things that might have occurred and deal with that. She hiccuped.

"Feel better?" he asked.

"No," she said, wiping her eyes with a corner of her sleeve. "But I think I'll live."

"Scary shit," he said.

Maggie nodded. "When he first walked in, he had the gun out," she said. "He whacked Arthur on the head with it and Arthur went right over backwards and fell on the floor. He didn't move and I thought he was dead at first."

The thought of that made her tear up again and she didn't speak for some time.

"Then he made everyone get in the front room," she continued, voice quavering. "He told me to call the cops and tell them to get Angelique over there, fast. Said he was going to start shooting us, one every half hour, if they didn't bring her to the center."

She stood up and fetched a tissue from the kitchen counter, coming back and sitting down next to Gus again. She blew her nose, loudly.

"Nothing happened for about an hour," she continued. "I could hear the sirens and the cars pulling up outside. I knew we were in a hostage situation. All I could think about was keeping the women safe. And then…" Her voice caught, becoming husky with emotion again. "And then I thought about you. And the baby." She wept again, covering her eyes with the tissue. "I kept telling myself 'It wasn't meant to end this way.'" She looked at Gus. "That's true, isn't it?" she asked. "We're supposed to love one another for years and years until we're both old and toothless. That's what's going to happen, right?" She looked at Gus with imploring eyes, red-rimmed.

"Maggie," he said, "I fully intend to be around to gum you into ecstasy when we're both ninety-two. Promise."

She laughed at that, laughed and cried a little more, and laughed again. She smacked him playfully on the shoulder.

"Gum me into ecstasy?" she said. "You're sick, you know that? I gotta rethink this whole thing now." But she turned to him, threw her arms around him and held him tight.

"And then you walked in," she said, her words muffled by his chest. "Holding the pizza box. I just about croaked right then. I didn't have time to warn the others. You just did your cave man thing and rescued all of us."

She looked at him with teary eyes. He made some cave man sounds, grunts and barks.

"I don't know how you do it," she said. "I don't know *why* you do it. But you're always there, protecting me. Protecting us. Wham, bam and he's down. Like it took two seconds."

"You don't wait around and talk," Gus said. "You gotta act. Get him first. Take him down. He's not expecting that. He had a gun, right? Thought he was cock of the walk. That's good. You can surprise him. He had no idea."

Maggie sipped her wine. "I don't know how you do it," she said again.

"I'm a cop, Mags," he said. "It's what we do."

"Is it always going to be like this?" she asked. "I mean, in the last two weeks, you've almost been run over by a car, been shot at in your station house, and now you faced some hoodlum with a gun and took him down."

"I left my cape in the car," he said. "I can go get it …"

"That's three times you could have been killed," she said, ignoring his attempt at levity. "And that's just in the last two, three weeks. What's it going to be like in the next twenty years? How many times will someone try to kill you or hurt you?" Her eyes began to water up again. "Or me. Or the baby. I don't know if I can do this, Gus."

"Do what?"

"Live in the constant fear that you can be killed," she said. "At any time. You pull some guy over for speeding, and he pulls out a gun and blasts away. In this crazy ass world, everyone has a gun. And they all want to shoot people like you. How can I live with that? I don't want to be a widow."

"Jeez, Maggie ..."

"What?" she said hotly. "Don't try to tell me it isn't true, or that I'm just being emotional or something. I hate that. And it is true. Do you know the statistics on how often a member of law enforcement is killed or seriously wounded on the job? Do you? Because I sure as hell do. When I started dating you, I looked it up."

Gus reached over to touch her, to reassure her. But she pulled away from his touch as if it was electric. She stood up suddenly and went back over to the kitchen counter. She refilled her glass from the wine bottle. He looked at her.

"And don't start in with the wine business," she said. "I've just had one of the most stressful days in my entire life. I'm going to drink some wine and if you don't like it, you can just go pound some sand."

She stood there, quivering with indignation and emotion. He sipped his beer, trying to let the emotional level in the room simmer down a bit. Right now, saying anything would be like tossing a lit match into a puddle of gasoline.

"Aren't you going to say anything?" she demanded, finally.

"Not much I can say, Mags," he said. "You are right. Being a cop is a dangerous job. Takes a certain amount of fatalism just to put on the uniform and show up for work. Anything can happen on any given day, and a lot of that includes stuff that can be very bad. We all know that. But we like to think that between our training and our instincts for dangerous situations, most of the time we manage to muddle through those situations without getting hurt."

"That's what you got?" she said. She looked incensed. "Your training and your instincts? All that stands between you and the grave? And you're asking me to bet on that? With my life and that of our child?" She wrapped a hand protectively across her belly. "That's a big ask, Gus. Real big. Maybe impossibly big. I just don't know …"

Gus finished his beer and stood up from the couch. He took his glass into the kitchen and washed it out, put it in the dish rack. He came back into the living room.

"Maggie," he said, "I'm a cop. My dad was a cop. It's in my blood. I could go get a job in some office, working in a cubicle eight hours a day. Would be safer, for sure. No one would be taking pot shots at me. I'd be safe. You'd be safe. Baby Huie there would be safe."

He stood right in front of her. Locked eyes. Hers were fearful. Questioning. Almost panicked.

"But I wouldn't be me. I'd hate every minute. I'm a cop. It's not a job, it's a calling. I'm called to protect and serve. It's what I do. I don't know what to tell you about how you can cope with that. You'll have to figure that out for yourself. Or talk to some other women who are married to police officers.

Maybe there's some coping skills. I don't know. But I do know what I am. And you know that too, by now."

He leaned over and kissed her, softly, on the lips.

"If you can't deal with that, I'll understand," he said. "It's not easy. I know that. And if you don't want to go through it, well, I'll try to live with that. Totally your call."

And then he turned and walked out the door.

CHAPTER 20

When Gus walked into the Little Penwick police station the next morning, everyone had heard the story on the news and greeted him like a hero. He didn't like that. He thought of himself as just a cop doing his job. Nothing particularly heroic about just doing your job.

Still, he smiled and thanked his officers as they came up to him to congratulate him for his successful intercession. He eventually made his way into the sanctum of his office. Jessica Martin came in with him.

"How's Maggie?" she asked.

Gus didn't answer at first, looking away uncomfortably.

"Uh-oh," she said. "What's wrong?"

"Maybe nothing," he said. "Maybe everything. The thing yesterday threw her for a loop."

"Understandable," Jessica said. "Would frighten anyone."

"So now she's reconsidering being married to a cop," he continued. "Sudden death lurking at every turn and all that. She's not sure she wants to go through all that. And doesn't think it's fair for the kid."

"Kid?" Jessica's eyebrows went up.

Gus nodded and smiled. "Oh, yeah. Maggie's expecting. Due in January. We were going to tell the family over the Fourth weekend. Fireworks to follow."

"Gus … that's wonderful news," Jessica said. Then she paused. "I mean, about the kid. It's terrible that she's feeling so vulnerable, of course. I imagine every spouse of a cop has feelings like that, at one point or another."

"Your Charley ever worry about you being a cop?" he asked.

She smiled. "I'm sure he has, in the past," she said. "It's a little different with me. Female officers aren't usually the first ones sent charging into dangerous situations. Not that women officers don't get involved in violence, ever. They do. But it's not quite the same."

She paused and studied his face. She thought he looked tired and a little worn down. It had been quite the eventful few weeks. She hoped all the stress he was showing wouldn't present itself in another PTSD episode. She worried about that. Then again, Gus Haddock had proved himself over and over, both as an Army Ranger in the worst of combat, and as a police officer here in Little Penwick. She did not think he was in any danger of losing his composure, no matter what happened.

"So where do things stand?" she asked.

Gus shrugged. "She's thinking about what she wants to do," he said. "I told her I would support whatever decision she reached."

"Would you really?" Jessica asked. "Would you let her go? You two are pretty awesome together, you know. You really seem to compliment each other in so many ways."

He nodded. "I thought so, too," he said. "We'll see what happens next."

Buzz Franklin stuck his head in the door to Gus' office.

"Just got a call from New Bedford, chief," he said. "They just picked up our driver. Wanted to know if we wanted to come down and talk to him."

"You bet," Gus said. "You drive."

"WHAT DO WE know about this guy?" Gus asked as Buzz drove east on I-195 towards the city of New Bedford, perched on the northern edge of Buzzard's Bay. The city had once been one of the whaling centers of the world — see Moby Dick by one-time resident Herman Melville — and while there was still an active commercial fishing fleet operating out of the downtown docks, the rest of the city had devolved into the usual post-Industrial malaise: empty brick factories, forests of three-story wooden tenements, lots of immigrants, lots of poverty, lots of crime.

"Name's Manual Diego," Buzz said. "Second generation immigrant from somewhere in Latin America, I forget where. He's known to be a member of a local gang called the Apaches."

"Isn't that cultural appropriation?" Gus said. "Hispanic gangbangers using a proud Native American name?"

"I'm sure it is," Buzz nodded, "And they probably don't give a pemmican's ass about it. Too busy boosting cars, huffing meth, spray-painting graffiti and shaking down shop owners."

"When did they pick him up?"

"Couple days ago," Buzz said. "New Bedford cops were keeping an eye on his girlfriend's place after we said we wanted to talk to Manny about the station shooting. Sooner or later, guys like Manny come sniffing around for a little sumthin-sumthin and that's when they grabbed him."

"He say anything yet?"

"Nah," Buzz shook his head. "He's pretending to be a quahog. All clammed up"

Buzz made his way into the city and pulled up outside the Ash Street Jail. That rickety old facility, in a three-story brick-towered building that took up much of the city block, was operated by the Bristol County Sheriff's Department. But it was where the New Bedford PD brought its prisoners before they were arraigned in court.

Inside, they checked in, left their guns with the deputy at the front desk and were ushered into an interview room. It was small and windowless, smelled like fear, with a metal table and four chairs anchored in the middle. They sat and waited, listing to the echoing sounds from the cells above: clanging gates, inmates shouting. Ten minutes later, the door opened and two deputies led Manny Diego in and shackled him to the table. One deputy stayed, standing against the wall behind Diego.

"Good morning, Mr. Diego," Buzz said once he had settled down in his chair. "I'm Detective Buzz Franklin and this is Gus Haddock, chief of police of the town of Little Penwick, Rhode Island. We have come here today to talk with you about the shooting incident at our police station on 17 June. We have evidence that shows you were one of the participants in that incident. Can you tell us why you helped Jack Ferro to shoot the front door out of our police station?"

Manny Diego was a large man, an inch or two over six feet and probably close to 300 pounds. His head was bald and shiny in the lights in the room. He was wearing the usual orange prison uniform, and Gus could see a web of tattoos crawling up his neck. His bare arms were covered in black and blue designs, with a little red thrown in. Gus couldn't tell what the designs were about. The words on his tattoos were mostly in Spanish and, Gus noted, what appeared to be German as well. Manny's hands, shackled in front of him, were the size of baked hams. His face was covered in several days' worth of beard and his small pinpoint eyes darted back and forth between Gus and Buzz.

"No comment," he said in heavily accented English.

"Can you tell us, please, about Janine Stone?" Gus said.

"Who dat?" Manny said.

"The woman who called you and offered you money to drive Jack Ferro to the police station where he fired fifteen rounds and injured one of my officers," Gus said, keeping his voice level and low. "Did you know her before she called you?"

"No comment," Manny said.

"Have you ever done work for someone named Ricardo Giancarlo?" Gus asked next.

"Ricky?" Manny said, eyes lighting up. "Si. Ricardo is the hermano."

"What kind of work have you done for this hermano?" Gus said.

Manny smiled. His teeth were brown and uneven. "I do lots of things," he said. "Debt collection, mostly."

"He pay you well?"

Manny smiled. "Si," he said. "Mucho dinero."

"When Janine Stone called you to do the Little Penwick job, did she tell you why she wanted the police station to be assaulted?"

Manny shook his head. "No," he said. "I think she said she was a friend of Ricky's."

"Did Ricardo call you and tell you she was going to call?"

Manny shrugged. Maybe. Maybe not.

"Was it Ricardo Giancarlo or Janine Stone who told you to steal a late-model GMC Acadia to use in this job?" Gus asked.

"No comment."

Gus looked across the table. "Mr. Diego," he said. "We have evidence that you were driving the stolen GMC Acadia which was used in the shooting incident at our station."

"Count one," Buzz said.

"That shooting incident resulted in an injury to one of the Little Penwick patrolmen who were inside the station at the time," Gus continued. "That's assault against an officer of the law in the commission of a felony crime."

"Count two," Buzz said.

"By your own admission, you were recruited for this job in conversations with one Ricardo Giancarlo of Providence, as well as with Ms. Janine Stone, address unknown, which is proof of a conspiracy to commit a felony with a firearm."

"Count three," Buzz said. "Three strikes and you're going away for fifty to life."

"Only if you prove it," Manny said, smiling at the two of them.

"Oh, we will, sir," Gus said. "Believe me, we will. Do you have anything further to say?"

Manny shook his head and looked down at his shackled hands.

Gus nodded at the deputy standing against the wall behind Manny, and he took the prisoner back to the cells. The door shut with a clang.

Before heading back to Little Penwick, Buzz drove them over to the commerical docks at Fisherman's Wharf, and they went into the Black Whale and took a table outside, under the tent, with views of the busy port. Gus ordered the lobster roll with celery, chives, lemon juice and mayo while Buzz asked for the sweet and sour Boom Boom Shrimp and a salad.

"So what have we learned?" Buzz asked rhetorically when the waitress had taken their orders and brought them each a tall glass of iced tea.

"We learned that Ricky Giancarlo keeps turning up wherever the lovely Janine is," Gus said. "Like they're connected at the hip. He was funding their little smuggling ring. He helped her find a goombah to shoot up the station. And I just learned yesterday that he's part of a business group up in the city that thinks they own Slate Evans, our local rock 'n' roll legend."

"Slate Evans of The Slayers?" Buzz asked. "I knew he came to town in the summer. Didn't hear that he was involved with Giancarlo."

"It's more the other way," Gus said. "Ricky owns a company that is aligned with another company that seems to have a pretty deep hook into both Slate and the other members of the band. He's ordered Slate to play a concert on the Fourth of July, and Evans wants no part of it. He came to me to ask what I could do."

"What can you do?"

"We have a noise ordinance," Gus said. "I'm going to take a look at it, maybe talk to Bob Murtha. I don't know what kind of live performance regulations the town has on the books. See what we can do."

"What about Manny?"

Gus shrugged. "Draw up the charges," he said. "We'll get him transferred up to our jurisdiction and set the wheels of justice in motion. Be interesting to see who turns up to represent him in court."

"You think Giancarlo will try to bail him out?" Buzz said.

"No question," Gus said. "Sounds like the two of them are good buddies."

"Always good to have a buddy when you need a leg broken," Buzz said.

"True," Gus said. "Not that I'd know. I don't have a good leg breaker in my phone contacts."

Buzz smiled. "You got me, chief," he said. "All the leg breakin' you'll ever need. You call, we haul, that's all."

CHAPTER 21

THE NEXT MORNING, Gus was finally beginning to make some headway on his paperwork. He made it through the requisition forms, approved overtime and vacation requests, and filed away a ton of things that needed filing. He stopped when he got down to the personnel folder at the bottom of his in box. He opened the folder and looked, again, at the files on each of the four candidates for the two openings he had. He took the file for one of the four and put it back in the in box. He'd deal with that one separately. He read through the other three carefully, one more time. He liked them all, but could only hire two.

He was thinking about that when he got a call on his cell. He didn't immediately recognize the number, but it showed as a local number, so he took the call.

"Chief Haddock?" a voice said. "This is the Big O, Ernie O'Connell. From the Star Riders club?"

"Sure, Ernie," Gus said. "Enjoyed lunch the other day. And I know our guest did as well. What can I do for you?"

"Yeah, it was quite the deal to have Slate in my place," he said. "It was very friendly of him to pick up the tab for everyone. I got a great shot on my phone of me and him. It's going on the wall once I get a poster-size copy printed out. Bring him back anytime." He paused and then spoke. "I'm calling because I'm worried about one of our former members, and one of our brothers," Ernie said. "My wife volunteers for the local Meals on Wheels group at the Congregational church. And she came home yesterday worried about one of her clients, guy named Jim McGinness."

"Coach Mac?" Gus said. "He lives on a farm over near the beach, right? Used to coach Little League teams?"

"Yeah, that's Coach," Ernie said. "He's well into his eighties now, and his heart is slowly giving out. Mind, too. Him and his missus live by themselves on their farm. They have no family to look out for them, which is why Angie, my wife, has them on her delivery route. Anyway, she came home last night and told me he's in pretty bad shape. She was wondering if there's anything you can do?"

Gus thought about that for a bit.

"He served in Korea," Ernie said. "Was attached to the 160th Infantry. Honorable discharge, like most of the fellas back then."

Gus was already thinking of the social services he could call in to help McGinness. Hearing that the man was a veteran of Korea, where Gus' own grandfather had fallen, reinforced his desire to do something to help the man.

"If I get involved, that might start him down a road he doesn't want to travel," Gus said. "I call Children and Family Services, or the state Elder Care office, they might come in, do an assessment and ship him off to a home somewhere. If that happens, there's nothing much I can do as chief of police. It'd be out of my hands. And if I recall, the McGinness's have farmed that land for three or four generations."

"I understand, Chief," Ernie said, "And I appreciate your concern. But from what Angie told me, it sounds like he really needs some help. She said the place looks like its falling down, gone to hell."

"OK," Gus said, "I'll stop over and see how he's doing."

"That would be excellent," Ernie said. Gus could hear the sound of relief in his voice. "Will you let me know what you find?"

"Sure thing, Ernie," Gus said. "Thanks for letting me know."

ABOUT AN HOUR later, Gus pulled into the short driveway next to a small wooden house, framed by a couple of old trees, about five hundred yards from the entrance to the town beach at Crescent Point. There was a hand-carved wooden sign over the front door that said McGinness. The house had a narrow screen porch in the front and was just one story. An old garage at the end of the drive looked like it had seen better days: it was leaning slightly to port and the doors were swung wide open and looked like they hadn't been shut for years. The inside of the garage was dark but with sunlight streaming in a small window on one side, Gus could see a riding mower and some other tools stacked against the wall.

He parked his SUV, got out and looked around. The small front yard was unkempt, with tufts of grass rising in uncut stalks and piles of leaves from last fall covering the walk. Gus walked up to the house, pulled open the screen door, hinges screeching in protest, and knocked at the front door, which had three small windows across the top. The door, and the house, were in need of a new coat of paint.

Gus heard someone moving around inside and heard a faint "hold on a sec" before the door finally opened. A tiny white haired lady stood there, peering out at Gus through rheumy eyes behind her thick glasses. She had a sharp nose, a pointed chin and sunken cheeks, and was wearing an old cotton house dress in a faded shade of blue, wooly pink slippers gripping her tiny feet.

"Miz McGinness?" Gus said. "I'm Chief Haddock from the Little Penwick police. May I come in?"

"We done somethin' wrong?" the old lady squeaked.

"No ma'am," Gus said. "I was just in the neighborhood and thought I'd stop in and see how Coach Mac is doing. Just here to say hello."

The old lady looked up at Gus' face, trying to recognize him. Failing that, she shook her head, smiled a bit and stood back, opening the door further and indicating Gus could come in. "Been a long time since I heard anyone call Jimmy 'Coach,'" she said. "Come in, come in."

It was dark and cool inside the house. The front third was the living area, with a sofa and two rocking recliners, a cocktail table and a big TV in the corner. The kitchen was behind that, on the right side of the house, and on the left a dark hallway led into the back, where Gus assumed the bedroom was. He could see a side door down the hall where he figured the bathroom was.

One of the recliners was occupied by an old bear of a man. Jim McGinness looked like someone who had once been tall and athletic and muscular. Now, his giant body was shrunken and withered. Only his head, wreathed in a magnificent mane of white, was still large-size. His skin was mottled and dry, his eyes looked up at Gus through a cloud of pain. Still, he managed something of a smile for his guest.

"Who the hell are you?" he croaked.

"Gus Haddock," the chief said. "I'm with the police."

"Haddock?" The old man's head came up from his chest, nodding. "Any relation to Chief Julius Haddock?"

"He's my Dad," Gus said. The little woman sat down on the sofa as if walking to the door and back had exhausted her completely. She folded her hands in her lap.

"Your Dad?" McGinness said. "Then you must be … ummm … wait a sec, I'll remember …"

"Gus," Gus said. "Gus Haddock. I'm now the chief of police. My Dad retired last year."

"Is that a fact?" McGinness said. "Retired? Hell, he's not old enough to retire, is he? He's my age!"

Gus smiled. "I think you got a few years on him, Coach," he said.

"Mebbe so," the old man said, "mebbe so." He gave Gus a lopsided grin. "I think I got a few years on most ever'body. Ha!"

"I remember when you coached in Little League," Gus told him. "You always coached the Giants. I remember you'd always have a big chaw of tobacco in your cheek. Us kids thought that was kinda funny. Gross, but funny."

McGinness tried to follow what Gus was saying, nodding here and there. But he looked confused. *Hard of hearing* Gus thought to himself.

"I coached the Little League here in town for twenty-two years," he said. "Always coached the Giants. They was my team. Lotta kids played on my team over twenty-two years, let me tell you."

"I was on the Indians," Gus said. "But I remember your team was always tough."

"Taught 'em the fundamentals," McGinness said. "That age, you don't get many Ted Williams types. Teach 'em how to catch, how to throw, how to hit, how to run the bases. How to play the game. Fundamentals. Then you just let 'em have some fun. No sense bein' a tough bastid. It was Little League in Little Penwick. Not the bigs. I got out when the parents couldn't understand that." He peered up at Gus, head cocked to one side. "What did you say your name was, sonny?"

"Gus," Gus said, a little louder this time. "Gus Haddock."

"Haddock," McGinness said, mostly to himself. "I knew someone named Haddock, once." He turned and looked at the little lady on the sofa. "Lizzie," he called loudly to her, even though she was four feet away, "Who did I used to know name of Haddock?"

The lady looked at Gus apologetically. "He has good days and bad ones," she said. "This one is right in the middle."

Gus decided to focus in on her. "He see a doctor on a regular basis?" he asked her.

"Oh, yes," she said. "Doc Harnett sees him once a year and if he gets the flu or something. And we go up to the VA in Providence from time to time."

"That's a long trip," Gus said.

"Oh, yes, it surely is," Lizzie said. "I always ask my cousin Frankie if he can drive us up there and back. I can't drive all that way myself anymore."

Gus nodded at her. "That's probably a good idea," he said. "You two getting enough to eat these days?"

Lizzie nodded. "Oh, yes," she said. "That lovely Angela from the church brings us a nice box of food twice a week. Usually it's already cooked and ready on a plate. All I have to do is heat it up. And she brings us nice fruit and sometimes a box of cookies or some chocolate."

"So you think you two are getting along okay?" he asked.

"Oh, sure," she said, nodding. "We do the best we can. We're both getting on in years. Only the Lord knows when one of us will get called home. But we manage. We still have each other."

"*Haddock*!" Jim McGinness practically shouted the name this time. Both Gus and Lizzie jumped. "Julius Haddock is chief of police. I knew I knew that name from somewheres." He sat back in his recliner, proud that he had remembered something.

Gus bent over and patted his arm. "You're right, sir," he said. "Julius Haddock was chief of police."

Jim's eyes glistened with pride. "I knew it," he said. "I knew that."

Gus smiled at the old man. Then he turned to Lizzie. "I'm going to take a quick look around the place," he said. "Then I'll come back in and talk to you. Okay?"

She nodded, hands folded in her lap. "That'll be fine, Gus," she said.

Gus went outside and walked around the house into the back. Once upon a time, Jim McGinness had farmed the land he owned, just like his father and grandfather before him. Looking now across the fallow fields, Gus estimated there were about ten acres in two fields separated by a row of trees and the ubiquitous stone wall. A two-track dirt road ran down through the fields next to the wall. At the far end of the field, Gus could see a cabin of some sort, partially hidden by the trees. The fields were overgrown with weeds, grasses and sedge. Still, Gus could tell the dirt underneath was rich and fertile. Someone had been farming this land since the late 1600s. There had been good years, when the harvest was rich and rewarding, and poor years, when the weather refused to cooperate, and the yields were low. The farmers who lived here ate well in the good years, and scrounged and saved when the harvests were bad. Farming was no game for sissies. Never had been.

Gus continued around the house. He checked the foundations to make sure they were sound, looked up at the roof and its gutters, which needed cleaning out, and noted that the previous autumn's load of fallen leaves had not been raked. He suspected Coach McGinness didn't get outside much anymore. He had seen enough.

He went back inside, knocking on the door and entering so Lizzie didn't have to get up from her place on the sofa again. The old man peered up at him.

"Who the hell are you?" he said.

Gus ignored him and spoke to Lizzie.

"Thanks for your time, Miz McGinness," he said. "I may have someone stop in for a visit with you in the next few days. They can probably help you get a few more resources so you can live here safely. Is that okay with you?"

"Oh, yes dear," she said. "We would appreciate any help we could get."

"Okay, fine," Gus said. Then he hesitated. "I saw a cabin or something out at the end of your field. Does that belong to you?"

"Oh, yes," Lizzie said. "Jim used it as a hunting cabin. He would dress the deer down there. I never liked to see those poor creatures all cut up and bleeding."

"Is there anyone using that cabin now?," Gus said.

"Oh, yes," Lizzie said, smiling at Gus. "We have a very nice young man who helps out with the yard work from time to time. His name is …" She paused, thinking. "Well, I can't quite remember his name. But he asked if he could use the cabin. He was planning on doing some hunting and saw Jim's deer hoist out there."

"When was that?" Gus asked.

"When was what?"

"When did he ask to use the hunting cabin?"

Lizzie thought about that, blinking her eyes rapidly.

"Why, it must have been during hunting season," she said finally.

"So, last fall sometime?" Gus asked.

"Why yes, I think that is right," she said.

"But you don't remember his name?"

Lizzie turned to Jim. His head had dropped down on his chest and he was resting his eyes.

"Jim, dear," she said, "What is the name of our yard man?"

"What?" he bellowed, head snapping up. "Yard man? What yard man? Do we have a yard man?"

"That's what I asked you," she said. "What is his name? Dave? Dick? Something that starts with a D. He's one of those Portuguese, lives over in the swamp. What is his name?""

"Danny?" Gus suggested.

"That's it!" Lizzie beamed with the accomplishment of remembering the name. "Danny. Danny Ferro. He is a nice man. Lives nearby. Very helpful. He was on one of Jim's teams, when he was a boy. Jim coached the Giants, you know.""

"Okay, Miz McGinness," Gus said. He knew if he didn't get out of this house, they'd start over again in the game of 'who the hell are you?' "I'll have somebody come out next week and see what they can do to help you two."

"Thank you Gus," Lizzie McGinness said, smiling up at him. "It was so nice to see you again."

Again? Gus thought. But he figured both of the McGinness couple faded in and out of reality, so he left it alone and backed out of the house, smiling and waving at the two of them.

CHAPTER 22

BACK IN THE office, Gus made a series of calls. The Elder Care division of the state Child and Family Services department had several options available for the McGinness couple. They could get home care and adult day care services, continue with their Meals on Wheels program, get counseling for depression and other medical needs and get help in maintaining their home. They also agreed to send out an insurance counselor to evaluate the McGinness' Medicare program benefits and see if they qualified for more care.

After talking with a counselor, the Division agreed to send a field officer out to interview the McGinness' in a few days. Gus asked if he could also be present at the interview, and the counselor agreed to notify him of the time and day of the appointment. Gus wanted to be there to make sure the McGinness couple wasn't given the runaround by an uncaring state official.

When he finally got off the phone, he called Buzz Franklin into his office. The chief of detectives ambled in and sat down.

"I heard you went out to see old Jimmy Mac," Buzz said. "He's probably coached more Little Penwick ball players than anyone in history. He doing okay?"

"Not really," Gus said. "I just spent an hour with Family Services, arranging for visits and talking about what they can and can't do for them. They're gonna send a counselor out next week to take a look at their situation. It's not pretty."

"Geez," Buzz said, "Remind me never to grow old."

"Right," Gus said. "Listen, we need to go back out to the McGinness place. You got some time right now?"

"Sure," Gus said, looking inquisitively at Gus. "What's up?'

"Missus Mac told me that a nice young man who some-times did yard work for them asked if he could use their hunt-ing cabin during last fall's season," Gus said. "After we tap danced around it for a time, they told me the young man was Danny Ferro."

"No shit?" Buzz said.

"Danny used to play for Jim with the Giants in Little League. But we need to take a look around out there, see what we can see."

"Aha," Buzz said, standing up. "The game is afoot. I'll get my car."

THE DAY WAS overcast, but warm and muggy, a foretaste of what was sure to come in July and August and on into September. When the temperatures rose, the ocean pumped in waves of humidity that quickly became unbearable.

Buzz drove them past the McGinness house and turned onto the dual track dirt road that ran next to the woods down to the far edge of the fallow fields. The old weathered cabin stood empty in a clearing between the row of trees and the open fields. Way off to the south, they could catch a glimpse of the sea, extending outward into eternity.

The cabin was just one small room, sitting on concrete blocks, with a wooden stoop across the front. There was a door and window in the front. The roof was steeply pitched so melting snow would slide off. Gus suspected the inside was open beams and plywood roof decking. The cabin did not appear to have any electricity or heat. In the old days, they'd call it a three-season house, because nobody would want to be inside it during the depths of winter.

The two officers looked around while sitting in the car. Neither could see anything that looked like tire tracks, but the ground was mostly grassy and firm. Out behind the cabin, towards the woods, was Coach McGinness' old deer rack, a tripod hoist made of thick metal tubing, with a heavy chain dangling down. You wrap up the deer's hind legs, hoist it into the air and cut open its belly, draining the innards and the blood into a metal tub. Then you could butcher the meat.

"That thing doesn't look like its been used for years," Buzz commented, nodding at the hoist.

"Yeah," Gus said. "So either Danny didn't have any success hunting last fall or he was lying to the McGinness' about what he wanted to use the cabin for."

They got out of the car. Gus approached the front door of the cabin carefully, looking at the ground for anything that might have been abandoned or tossed aside. As he neared the front entrance, he pulled his gun. Buzz did likewise.

Gus knocked on the door. There was no answer. It was rather obvious that there was no one inside or anyplace around. Gus took a few steps and peered inside the grimy front window. The inside of the place was as he imagined: empty, save for a wooden table and small chair. It looked like there was a candle on the table, burned down to about six inches, with pools of melted wax collected at the base. The walls were tongue-and-groove slats and, as he had guessed, the ceiling was open to the beams. No kitchen, no bathroom. Most hunting cabins in these parts didn't have them. You would cook the meat on an open fire outside and if you had to pee, well, that's what the woods are for.

Gus turned back to the door and tried the handle. It opened. There was no lock. He pushed the door open and stuck his head inside. In the humid heat of the day, the air inside was thick and quiet. He could hear a faint buzzing, but wasn't sure if the insects making the noise were inside or out. He went in, holstering his gun. There was nobody here.

He looked around inside. The cabin was roughly fifteen feet square, so that didn't take very long. The floor was dusty and Gus could clearly see some footprints.

"Looks like someone has been here," Gus said, "But it's hard to tell if they've been here recently or years ago."

"I'll call the state forensics boys, have them come down," Buzz said. "They can photograph those footprints and maybe they'll get lucky and pick up a print or two."

Gus nodded. "Let's take a look around outside," he said. The cabin stood about fifteen yards from the edge of the woods that extended all the way back to Crescent Beach Road. The stand of trees and scrub was about ten yards across, serving as a natural windbreak between McGinness' two fields.

Gus and Buzz each took one side of the cabin and began a slow walk back towards the woods, looking for cigarette butts, Coke cans, sandwich bags … anything that might be tied back forensically to a human being. Gus couldn't see anything as he slowly paced back and forth. It was all just grass, dead leaves, sticks and dirt.

Buzz finished surveying his half of the yard first, and stepped into the wooded area, brushing aside the prickly undergrowth and saplings that were growing around the bases of the taller, well established oaks and poplars. Gus turned around and started walking slowly back towards the cabin, eyes glued to the ground, looking for anything out of the ordinary.

"Chief!" Buzz called from the woods. "Better come see this."

Gus followed the pathway Buzz had created by pushing through the scrub. About twenty feet in from the edge of the woods, he had found a circular structure of rocks and stones, haphazardly stuck together with concrete. A large square piece of steel plate lay on top of the circular wall.

"Looks like an old well," Buzz said. "Most of these old places had wells." He looked around. "I don't know why they'd dig one this far from the road, unless they used the water to irrigate the fields. Or maybe the main house was once located out here, not back there by the street. Historical Society would know. They've got all the plat records going back three hundred years."

"Let's get this cover off," Gus said.

It took both of them, straining and pushing, to lift up the steel plate and move it, inch by inch, off the stones. When they had moved it out of the way, there was indeed a deep black hole extending down into the ground. Gus pulled out his cell phone and turned on the flashlight feature, but his light only reached down about five feet. The well went deeper than that.

"Let me go get my big light," Buzz said, and he went back to his car to retrieve a flash light from his truck. It was a twelve-inch tactical light in a black aluminum case.

"I forget how many lumens this thing has," he said when he got back to the well. "But it beats the hell out of your cell phone. And if we run into any bad guys, it's pretty useful for beating the hell out of them, too."

He clicked it on and shone the light down into the inky depths of the well. They could see the walls of the well had been carefully built with bricks and mortar. Someone had put in a lot of effort. The brick was darkly stained with time and some roots and vines had taken hold in the mortar and were trying to find a way to live in the near darkness. Buzz leaned over the edge and pointed his light straight down.

"   Ah," he said. "Lookee there."

Gus leaned over too, holding Buzz' shoulder for support and gazed down into the well.

About thirty feet down the shaft of the well, he could see the light reflected in the surface of the black water. But just below the surface was a boxy shape. It looked to be about three feet square and there was a length of chain — about six feet in length — bolted on each side to the box.

"Looks like a chain handle," Buzz said. "On the side of a metal box of some kind."

"I wonder what's inside," Gus said, pulling himself back from the edge and standing up.

"Maybe we can use that old deer rack and pull 'er out of there," Buzz said. "I've got some chain and some heavy duty rope in the car."

IT TOOK THEM the better part of two hours. They wrestled the hoist in place atop the well, dropped a line down into the water and, after several unsuccessful attempts accompanied by some inventive cursing, they finally managed to hook the chain handle on the sunken box and, with both of them straining on the rope, finally hauled the heavy box out of the well and got it back on terra firma.

The box was about two feet wide and three feet deep, made of some kind of alloy aluminum. The top of the box, the side that had the chain handle, was affixed to the rest of the box with four large stainless screws with thick rubber washers.

"Looks pretty waterproof," Buzz said as they examined the box. "I'll bet there's a gasket inside this lid. Whoever made this thing knew what they were doing."

"Someone told me that Danny Ferro was pretty inventive with metals," Gus said. "I'm thinking he could have made a box like this in twenty minutes or less."

"Wonder what's inside," Buzz said, winking at Gus.

"Well, before we open it, we need to document the scene," Gus said. "Let's get some photographs."

They spent a half hour photographing the well, the hoist and the box in detail. Then, Buzz backed his car up to the edge of the woods and together they carefully lifted the box and carried it to the car. They both wore nitrile gloves to keep their fingerprints off the box — the forensics guys would want to try to pull some prints.

Once the box was firmly seated in the back shelf of Buzz' SUV, Gus found a large screwdriver and backed out the four corner screws holding the lid on. When the last one came out, he used the screwdriver to pry the lid off the base. It finally separated with a slight puff of compressed air. Gus lifted it off and set it to one side.

Inside the box were bricks and bricks of cash, wrapped in paper and sealed with rubber bands. Each brick was about three inches thick. Gus rifled the edge of one brick. Mostly hundreds.

"Where's the freakin' rainbow?" Buzz said, his voice hushed in amazement.

"How's that?"

"We just found the pot of gold at the rainbow's end, Chief," Buzz said. "This is the money Janine's been looking for."

CHAPTER 23

BACK AT THE station, Gus and Buzz worked late into the night. They carried the metal box into the conference room and began counting. Each one would remove a brick of currency from the box, unwrap it, count the bills, write down the amount, re-wrap the brick in paper and rubber bands and put it aside, marked as counted.

They were an hour into the process when Jessica Martin stuck her head in the door. She saw what they were doing and whistled softly.

"Dang," she said. "Just keep in mind that Mama needs a new pair of shoes, just in case a couple of those benjamins falls on the floor or something."

"Mama could get a pretty nice new house, with all of this," Gus said, indicating the stacks of currency bricks. "You don't want to stay and help?"

"I would," Jessica said, "But my husband is taking me out for dinner over in Newport."

"What's the occasion? Buzz asked.

Jessica shrugged. "I don't know," she said. "Tuesday?"

"Have fun," Gus said, and she left.

They finished counting at around nine o'clock. Buzz called up a calculator app on his phone and began tapping in the last of the numbers. He looked at the screen and whistled.

"Six hundred and forty-two grand," he said. "Give or take a hundred or three."

"This is the money Janine has been looking for," Gus said. "She's gonna have a hissy if she finds out we have it."

"And I'd love to be the one to tell her," Buzz said. "Just to see the expression on her face."

"Me, too," Gus said. "But I think we should keep this news under wraps. Chances are that Janine will poke her head up sooner or later if she's still looking for the money."

"I'll put it in the safe," Buzz said. "Mum's the word."

He was in the car, about halfway back to his garage apartment, when his cell rang.

"Gus?" a female voice said, "It's me."

"Hey, Mags," he said. "How are you feeling?"

"Freaked and freaky," she said. She paused. "I wish you were here."

"I'd come up," he said, "But it's been a long day. I'm heading back to the apartment. I need some sleep."

"I understand," she said. "It's a long way."

"Feels like about a million miles," he said. "I don't like that."

"I know," she said. Her voice sounded small. "I-I'm sorry for the things I said yesterday."

"It's OK, Mags," he said. "You went through a lot. Enough to jolt anyone."

"What are we gonna do?"

He was silent. He arrived at Mrs. P's place, pulled in next to the garage and killed the engine. It was deep twilight, with just a weak glow on the western horizon. Looking up, he could see stars.

"I wish I knew," he said finally. "But I don't. So I guess we'll just have to figure it all out for ourselves."

"I love you, you know," she said.

"I know you do," he replied. "And I love you too."

"That's good," she said.

"And that's why we'll be able to figure it out," he said. "It's kinda meant to be."

"You think?"

"I do," he said.

There was a long silence. "I don't feel as freaky as I did a minute ago," she said.

"That's progress," he said. "Tomorrow will be better, too. And that day after that even better."

"You promise?"

"I promise."

"Okay," she said. "Sleep tight."

"And don't let the bedbugs bite."

"You have bedbugs?"

"Don't think so," he said. "It was something my Mom used to say to us when she put us to bed."

She laughed. "Mine, too," she said. "Parents are whack, aren't they?"

"Wonder what Junior will think about us some day."

"He'll think he had the best daddy in the world," she said.

"And the best mom."

"You think?"

"I do."

"Okay," she said. "Go get some sleep. And call me in the morning."

Inside his apartment, Gus got a beer out of the fridge, sat down on his sofa and dialed some numbers on his phone. He took a gulp of beer while it rang.

"Yo? Junior? That you?"

"Hi Dad," Gus said. "Not interrupting anything, am I?"

"This time of night?" his father said. ""Nah. I'm watching the Sox bullpen completely disintegrate. Y'know, these guys are all highly trained athletes, right? They've all come up through college ball or the minors. They've been successful pitchers, which is why the Sox agreed to throw unGodly amounts of money at them. You would think one of them would be able to throw a couple strikes, get someone to hit a ground ball or a pop up. But no. Walk, single, wild pitch, double, dinger… So they bring in the next guy, and it's the same goddam thing! It's like they come out of that bullpen in right field and walk through a brain cloud or something and forget everything they ever knew about pitching. It's the god-damnedest thing."

Julius stopped and took a breath.

"But you probably didn't call me for a Sox update and rant," he said. "What's up?"

"Girl trouble," Gus said.

"Maggie?"

"Yeah."

Julius paused. "Heard about that thing up in Providence," he said. "Nice work, by the way. Just like I taught you. Move fast, take 'em by surprise." He paused again. "She having trouble dealing with all that?"

"A bit," Gus said. "But she's now wondering why she's involved with a cop. The danger. The worry about being shot and stuff. Getting that call at 2 a.m. and all that."

"Ah," Julius said. "Well, I suppose it's good she's thinking about all this stuff before you two get in too deep."

"Yeah," Gus said, "I think we're past that point."

"Oh?" Julius said. "Well, that's good. I like Maggie. Has a good head on her shoulders, for a lawyer."

"How do you get past this part?" Gus said. "How did Mom deal with … with you're being a cop and all? Or Siggi?"

Julius chuckled.

"I told your mother, morning after we got hitched, that I wouldn't allow myself to get hurt on the job," he said. "Because I knew if I did, she'd kill me."

Gus laughed. "So she learned to deal with it?"

"Don't know, son," his father said. "We didn't talk about it that much. I think she just got used to what I did for a living. Of course, here in Little Penwick, there aren't bullets flying overhead at all hours of the day. It's different in other towns, other places. But she knew police work was inherently dangerous. Every now and then, there'd be an incident somewhere in the state, or over in Massachusetts. Cop'd get his ticket punched. She'd always make sure my dress uniform was pressed and ready. Help me suit up. Make me go to the funeral. 'It's important you go pay your respects,' she'd tell me. "

He paused. Gus could hear the television announcers in the background, talking about the Sox.

"I always wondered if, by making me go to all those other funerals, she was hoping Karma would be on my side, if it ever came to something happening here," he said. "I guess that was one way she dealt with it all."

"And Siggi?"

"You can ask her yourself," Julius said. "She's gone to bed right now, but you can talk to her whenever you want. Maybe Maggie should talk to her, too. When is she coming down for a weekend?"

"I think she'll be here for the Fourth," Gus said.

"You think?"

"Still a little up in the air," Gus said. "She's pretty upset."

"Ahh," Julius said. "Okay, then. We'll hope to see her on the Fourth. Hamburgers, hot dogs, apple pie and cop shop talk."

"Don't forget the fireworks," Gus said.

"Those will take care of themselves," his father said. "Speaking of which, how's your other girlfriend problem?"

"Janine?" Gus said. "I think we found the stash of money she was looking for. We've popped both of the lugs who shot up the station. She paid for it. But they say they don't know where she is. But I expect her to come out in the open pretty soon. She needs the cash, and now I've got it."

"Keep your eyes open," Julius said. "A cornered animal is the most dangerous."

"But they're only thinking about escape," Gus said. "Which gives me the advantage."

"Hope so," his father said. "Just watch your back."

"Always do," Gus said. "Always do."

"One more thing," Julius said.

"What?"

"You took Slate Evans to lunch at the Star Riders Club and didn't call me?" His father was trying to keep a note of whining out his voice. But he failed.

"Yeah," Gus said. "He called me to come pick him up. Happened fast. Didn't have time to call." He paused. "How did you hear about that?"

His father chuckled. "Son, this is Little Penwick. It's an old Wampanoag word that means 'There are no secrets.'"

"I didn't know you were a fan," Gus said.

"Fan?" Julius sounded amazed. "Sonny boy, everyone, especially those of my particular age, who went through Viet Nam and the Summer of Love and Woodstock and all of that … we've got a soundtrack to our lives. And Slate Evans and The Slayers were a big part of my soundtrack. Hell, if I remember correctly, I lost my virginity to your mother to the sound of Forever Love. Jocko Morgan singing that ballad, Slate playin' that riff before the chorus."

Julius began to sing. "*I'll love you forever. Forever and a dayyyyy.*"

"Geez, Dad," Gus said. "That's way too much information. But I'll invite you to the next lunch meeting I have with Slate."

"You better," his father said. "Or I'll come over to your office and start singing all their greatest hits."

"Please don't," Gus said. "I just replaced the glass in the door."

CHAPTER 24

GUS CALLED A staff meeting for ten. Jessica Martin and Buzz Franklin brought coffee with them when they walked in.

"Okay," Gus said when they settled in. "We've got Janine's money in our safe. She doesn't know that. And so far, we haven't heard from her in at least a week or so."

"What's our next move?" Jessica asked.

Gus thought about that for a minute or so, fiddling with a rubber band. He paused and looked at his two officers. "What if we tell her we've got it?"

Buzz and Jessica looked at each other. Then they turned back and looked at Gus.

"Uh, boss?" Buzz said. "If you remember, that woman hired two people to shoot our front door out. We never really found out why."

"She told young Jackie that he needed to avenge his family name," Gus said. "I don't know what she told Manny Diego. I don't think it mattered. That guy was more interested in the cold hard cash she gave him. Didn't give a crap about the reason why."

"But what I think Buzz is saying," Jessica said, "Is that if she finds out you've got her money in our safe, she's gonna come after it. And if she'll tell two local idiots to shoot out our door just for the jollies, what is she gonna do if she gets really serious?"

"Small tactical nuke?" Gus said with a smile.

"Or the local Janine equivalent," Buzz said. "It would put this station and everyone in it at risk. Me, you, everyone."

"Unless we can thwart her and put her in jail," Gus said. "We're the police, after all. Thwarting is what we do best."

"Buzz might be right," Jessica said. "The risk-reward ratio might not tilt in our favor."

"So the safe thing to do is to sit on the money," Gus said. "How do we pick up Janine?"

"If she's snooping around looking for her stash, she's sure to turn up somewhere," Jessica said. "Law of averages says we'll get her eventually."

Gus looked at Buzz, eyebrows raised in question. Buzz stared back for a moment, then smiled.

"I think I'm finally getting on your wavelength, chief," he said. "What Jessica says — don't let on that we have the money, wait for the girl to show her face — that's the safe, common-sense way to handle it."

Gus nodded, indicating Buzz should continue.

"But you're not one for the safe and the common sense," Buzz continued. "That's the way everyone expects the chief of police to be — safe and secure and right down the middle. Don't rock the boat. Follow the law. But Gus Haddock doesn't play things safe. He goes in to a crowded storefront full of women held hostage by a knucklehead, carries in a pizza and slam-bam-thank-you-ma'am, he grabs the gun and takes the guy down."

"Wasn't quite like that, but you're in the ballpark," Gus said. "Go on."

"So in this case, we tell everyone we have all that money in our safe," he said. "Don't have to link it to Janine. Just tell the world we found six hundred grand. Say it was a drug bust or something."

"That way, we can keep it all," Jessica said. "Just like when Chief Julius busted that drug mule with a Chevrolet full of money ten, fifteen years ago. Paid for this building."

"And a portion of both your salaries," Gus said. "And mine."

"Wait a minute," Buzz held up a hand in protest. "Do we really get to keep that money? I mean, it was located on the McGuiness property. Aren't they in line for at least a portion of those funds?"

Gus nodded. "Good point," he said. "I'll ask our town's legal beagle to research the matter. It might be that we split it with the McGuiness's."

"They could certainly use the money," Jessica said, nodding her agreement with that idea.

"But when Janine hears about our windfall, she'll know that the money we found belongs to her," Buzz continued. "And she'll come after it."

"How?" Jessica asked.

Buzz shrugged. "I don't know," he said. "She's pretty resourceful. Connected to those guys up in Providence."

"But the point is, she'll try something," Gus said. "And when she does, we'll be ready."

"You've got a plan," Jessica said. "See? I'm starting to figure you out too, chief. What have you come up with?"

Gus smiled. His brain trust was finally beginning to use their brains. "That's why I called this meeting," he said. "Here's how I think we can play this."

And, leaning forward, arms on his desk, he told them.

About a week later, Gus got back to the station around eleven. He had spent the morning at the end-of-year graduation ceremony at the Hilda Jane Boxford Elementary School. Named after a turn-of-the-Twentieth-Century schoolmarm who had overseen the education of Little Penwick's children in her one-room school, the Boxford School invited parents and friends of all the students to the end of year ceremony honoring those younger students who were moving up a grade, and to bid farewell to the eighth graders who, in September, would be riding the bus early every morning over to Portsmouth High. Gus had been one of the town officials on hand, along with three of the five town councilmen, including Bob Murtha, the council president.

The school band had played everyone out of the auditorium with a tinny sounding Sousa march, there were cookies and lemonade under the tree in the playground and then everyone went home, and Gus got back to work.

Jamie McMaster, on front desk duty, told Gus he had a visitor waiting in his office. Gus shot him an inquiring look.

"John King," Jamie said. "Security guy for Slate Evans."

Gus nodded and walked into his office. King had been sitting in one of the guest chairs in front of the chief's desk, and he stood up and smiled.

"Chief Haddock," he said, sticking out his hand. "John King. We met a week or so ago at Slate's house." King was oversized with a body that had obviously spent a lot of time in a gym somewhere, lifting weights and doing squats. He wore a black T-shirt that showed off his massive arms, thickly muscled chest and no-neck. His blondish hair was cut short in a military-type cut, shorn in back and on the sides, with a little extra left to decorate the top of his head. He had a deep forehead, strong chin and eyes that seemed to be glinting against a bright light.

"Mr. King," Gus said, shaking the guy's hand and sitting down at his desk. "What can I do for you?"

"I've got a few documents here that the folks over at City Hall said needed your John Hancock," he said. "We're doing a little backyard concert on the Fourth at Slate's place, inviting a hundred or so special guests."

He reached into a briefcase at his feet, pulled out some papers and handed them across the desk. Gus took them and began to read through them. He did this slowly, as if he was studying them for the first time. Actually, Bob Murtha had called Gus several days earlier to tell him that Narragansett Talent of Providence was applying for a waiver on the town's live performance ordinances. Specifically, Narragansett wanted to hold their concert in a non-commercially zoned location, to wit, Slate Evans' back yard; and to allow the live music to be played past the town's 9 p.m. limit. And, they wanted to have a fireworks show after the concert. As chief of police, Gus was required to sign off on the waiver application, in effect saying that the Little Penwick Police Department was fine with the event.

"How many guests will be attending?" Gus asked when he had finished reading through the pages.

"I don't have a final count," King said, "But it will be no more than 250."

"Have you notified the neighbors?" Gus asked next. "Ordinance says you are required to inform all abutting property owners that the event is scheduled. Give them time to register any complaints with the council and the zoning office."

King smiled. "We've done better than that," he said. "We've hand-delivered invitations to all six property owners on Slate's street to have them join us. Five of the six are planning to attend. The last one said she'll be out of town that night."

Gus nodded and made a note on one of the pages.

"Who's playing?" Gus asked next.

"Well, Slate himself will be the headliner," King said. "Instead of the members of The Slayers, he'll be joined by some rock musicians from Providence and Boston. I've got a list of them here ..." He went fishing in his briefcase again and pulled out the sheet listing the musicians.

"Ordinance says no live music outdoors after nine," Gus said.

"That's why we're applying for a waiver," King said. "We thought they could play up to around ten, and then we'll have the fireworks over the river."

"You got a permit for that part?" Gus asked. "The fireworks?"

"Yessir," King said. He brought out the fireworks permit and passed it to Gus.

Gus took it, nodded and began to read through the papers again. He read slowly, his brow furrowed. Once or twice, he stopped, went back to the previous page and pretended to re-read something. Gus was going to move his lips as he read, but thought that might be overkill.

He stopped reading, looked up at the ceiling, then continued, sighing loudly.

King watched all this with a wry smile on his lips. He clearly thought he was in the presence of a country bumpkin chief who was lost outside the pages of his speeding ticket book.

"You know chief," he finally said, "I know that Slate would be happy to have you come join us on the Fourth. He's always said how much he appreciates and supports law enforcement."

Gus looked up and grinned. "Really?" he said, his voice excited. "He'd do that?" He stopped, thinking. "Say, do you suppose it would be okay if I brought my Dad? He's been a huge Slayers fan his entire life. Made me and my sister listen to their albums when we were kids."

"Sure, sure," King said, nodding. "Bring the old man. We'd love to have him."

"Wow, that's great," Gus said happily. He bent back to the papers and resumed reading, one line at a time, as slowly as he could. Finally, when he figured he had drawn the thing out as long as he could, he reached for a pen and signed the papers. He stacked them up and handed them back to King.

"Now," Gus said, "I got a few questions for you. What about parking? If you get two hundred guests, where are they gonna put their cars?"

King nodded as if he had been expecting the question.

"Slate has got a field up north of his house that can hold about a hundred cars," he said. "We will direct arriving guests to park there."

"And the rest?"

King shrugged. "We have received word that a number of guests will be arriving by boat," King said.

Gus looked at him and raised his eyebrows.

"Most of the musicians for this concert are being provided by a record label up in Providence, Narragnsett Talent," King said. "We've received word that they are bringing a bunch of people down to the party on a boat owned by the principal of that record label."

"A hundred people on a boat?" Gus said. "That must be a pretty big boat."

King nodded. "Yes," he said, "The MusicNote is a good-size vessel. Two hundred feet in length."

Gus whistled. "Where in the hell are you gonna put that?" he said. "I'm not sure it'll fit inside the harbor, unless you tie her up at a mooring. But then you gotta move a hundred people off the boat and get them over to Slate's place. Sounds like a logistical nightmare."

"They intend to tie up at Slate's jetty," King said.

"Ah, yes, the jetty," Gus said. "Can it handle a yacht that size?"

"No problem, chief," King said. "We measured. She'll fit."

Gus stood up. "Well, it sounds like you've got everything under control Mr. King," he said, shaking his hand again. "I look forward to coming to the concert. Do you want me to assign some officers to handle crowd control and traffic on the night?"

King shook his head. "Don't think that'll be necessary, chief," he said. "But thanks for the offer. I've got my assistant and we'll have a few others coming down from Providence to help provide security, traffic and crowd control."

Gus nodded. "Perfect," he said. He started to escort King out of his office, but in the hallway, he stopped, held up his hand.

"Wait a sec," Gus said. "I should probably make copies of those permits. Just for our records." He led King into the bullpen and back to Buzz Franklin's office.

"Buzz," he said, leading into Franklin's office. "Can you make me some copies? This is John King, one of Slate Evans security guys. They're planning a little backyard concert on the Fourth."

"Really?" Buzz said. "Cool. Love the Slayers."

King fumbled around in his briefcase and took out the papers that Gus had just signed. "Actually, it won't be the whole band," he said. "Just Slate and a few friends."

"Oh," Buzz said, sounding disappointed. "Well, I'll get these copied in a jiffy."

He went off to the copy machine in the bullpen, leaving King and Gus standing outside his office. King looked around.

"How many officers are on the job, chief?" he asked.

"We got ten, plus three supervisors," Gus said. He smiled. "It's a small town. Not much going on. Unless you count the odd rock star concert on the Fourth."

King chuckled. "Glad we could provide some interest," he said.

Buzz came back and handed King the papers. "Here ya go," he said.

"Put our copies in the safe, Buzz, would ya?" Gus said.

"Sure thing, chief," Buzz said. He went over to the wall safe behind his desk, spun the knob on the front of the safe, went back and forth three times with the dial and popped the heavy door open. Inside, Gus and King could see stacks of currency piled inside.

King whistled. "You just solve the Great Train Robbery, chief?" he said. "That looks like a lotta cash."

Gus looked at the safe and chuckled. "Nah," he said. "That's evidence for a case coming up soon. Keeping it safe so we can show the jury."

"Right." King stuffed the papers back into his briefcase and shook hands with both Buzz and Gus. "I won't take up any more of your time, gentlemen," he said. "Thanks, chief."

They watched as King left the building. They waited a minute or two to make sure he had gone.

"Well, well, well," Buzz said. "Isn't that interesting?"

"Yeah," Gus said. "When Slate Evans told me that the Narragansett Talent outfit was run by our old friend Ricky Giancarlo, I knew something was up."

"And Mr. King will go back and tell Ricky that we've got a safe stuffed with cash," Buzz said.

"And Ricky will tell his old friend Janine Stone," Gus said.

"Which means there's really going to be fireworks this year on the Fourth of July," Buzz said.

"Hope so," Gus said. "We're planning on it."

CHAPTER 25

Julius Haddock walked through the door of the Sunrise Center for Women and came face-to-face with Arthur Manville, sitting behind his card table just inside the door.

"Hep you?" Arthur said.

"Is Maggie Wells here?" Julius said.

Arthur looked him over. "Who can I say is asking?" he said.

"Julius Haddock. I'm the father of her, um, main squeeze."

Arthur smiled at that. He nodded. "I'll tell her you're here," he said. He went into the office in the back, off the long room. After a short time, he came back out, followed by Maggie.

"Julius," she said in greeting, looking a bit surprised. "What brings you up to Providence?"

He leaned over and kissed her cheek. "Oh, I had some business up here," he said. "Tracking a couple of deadbeats for one of my clients. Thought I'd stop by and see if I could buy you some lunch."

Maggie glanced at her watch. It was about quarter to noon. She nodded. "Give me five minutes and I'll be ready," she said. She went back into her office. Julius smiled at Arthur. "Things quiet around here now that whass-is name is in jail?"

Arthur nodded. "Yassir," he said. "Pretty quiet on the whole."

"Good, good," Julius said. He sat down in a chair at the edge of the long room. Two black women were sitting at the end of the sofa, heads together, whispering, as they filled out a form on a clipboard.

"OK, Julius, let's go." Maggie came back out of her office, a leather bag thrown over her shoulder. Julius noted that she had freshened up her makeup and lipstick, brushed her hair back. "Where do you want to go?"

"What's good around here?" Julius asked. "I'm the stranger in town."

Arthur smiled. "Y'all might try Miss Daisy's," he said. "Next block over." He nodded in the general direction. "Her fried chicken can't be beat. Butter beans. Collards. Cornbread. Mmm. Makin' myself hungry just thinkin' 'bout it."

"You want us to bring you back a plate, Arthur?" Maggie said.

"Why, that would be most congenial of you, Miz Maggie," he said. He stood up and reached for his wallet. "Lemme give you some money …"

"No worries," Julius said. "It's on me. My treat."

"Well, thank you most kindly," Arthur said.

Julius and Maggie walked around the corner and found the restaurant about halfway down the next block. They could smell the fried chicken cooking in hot lard before they arrived at the raggedy storefront. Pushing inside, they found a long formica counter with some stools, and a few wooden tables next to the windows in front. A very large black woman sat behind the counter next to a large cash register. Julius figured she was Miss Daisy. A pass-through window behind her showed the kitchen, where two were working. One was keeping a close eye on the deep-fat fryer, where batter-dipped pieces of chicken were turning golden brown. The other cook was working on a table and cooktop where the sides were being prepared.

They took one of the tables and, after glancing at the menu, ordered two chicken dinners. Julius ordered his with fries and slaw, while Maggie opted for the beans and collard greens as her sides. Maggie asked Miss Daisy to add one more dinner to the order, to go. They each had a large red plastic glass of iced tea.

"So," Maggie said when they settled in at the table, "Gus send you up to talk to me?"

Julius smiled. "Talk to you about what?" he said. "I just thought we could have lunch together."

She looked at him, eyes narrowed. "Yeah, I'm not buying the innocent just dropped by thing," she said. "Your being up here in Olneyville isn't a coincidence. What do you want?"

"Ouch," Julius said. "I thought you had turned into a do-gooder. But it seems like you're still a lawyer. Suspicious. And direct."

Maggie didn't say anything. She sipped some tea and waited.

"Junior did call me the other night," Julius said. "Said you were having some second thoughts about being involved with a policeman. Worried about him getting shot or injured in some way on the job."

"I've read the statistics, Julius," Maggie said. "They're not pretty."

Julius smiled. "You ever hear that old saying? There's 'lies, damned lies and statistics.'"

"Meaning what, exactly?" Maggie retorted. "You're saying the statistics are lies? That policemen aren't sixty-three percent more likely to be shot on the job than, say, a factory worker? Sixty-three percent, Julius. That's a lot."

"Policing is a dangerous job, Maggie," Julius said. "No question about it. And it's not just getting shot that's a worry. Cops get run over, they get punched, kicked, knifed, beaten with bats and clubs, bitten by dogs and barfed on by drunks." He paused, looking at her. "And do you know why?"

She was silent.

"It's because it's a goddam dangerous job, that's why," he said. "But the people who do it, who sign up for the job, they do that because they want to. They want to help people who need help. There's nobody else who'll run into burning buildings or step between two people who are fighting, or jump into a cold ocean to save someone who's drowning. And if we don't have people willing to do all that, and more, who will?"

He paused, sipped some tea. She still sat silent, looking at him with her big brown eyes.

"It's not a job, Maggie," Julius continued. "It's a calling. It's a duty. Somebody has to be there to clean up the crap parts of our society. Somebody has to clap the cuffs on the bad guys. It's hard. It's not always fun. You get to see the worst of people and the worst in people. But you go to work every day expecting to help someone and you go home at night every night thinking you made a contribution. That's why we do it."

"And what if you come home dead?" she said. "All that high-falutin' bullshit about serving and protecting isn't worth crap if you end up on a slab. Because if Gus ends up on a slab, he can't protect me. Or …"

She stopped. Her eyes welled up. She sipped some tea.

"Or what?"

"Or the baby that we've created," she said finally. She looked directly into his eyes. *What about that?* she seemed to throw in his face.

Now Julius was silent for a time. He had suspected that Maggie was pregnant. He could see slight changes in her face, as well as that particular glow that people always talked about. He was excited about this news, of course, but he also understood how that could affect Maggie's attitude and thought process. She was already thinking about the baby, how to protect it, nurture it, help it grow. And she, naturally, wanted assurance that her partner would be there throughout to make it easier.

He reached over and took her hand. "Congrats, Mags," he said. "I mean that. You two will make a great family." He let her hand go. "But Junior is a cop, first and always. He's a little impetuous. That's his age. I remember when I was his age. Thought I could conquer the world. He'll learn. You usually do. But he's a cop. That's never going to change."

"So where does that leave me?" she asked. "Me and our baby? We just have to suck it up? Live with the idea that on any given day, Gus can walk out the door and never walk back in again? I just don't think I can live with that. I really don't."

Julius looked at her. "Couple days ago, some guy held a gun to your head. Literally. Now I don't know what the statistics say about how many women's counselors get shot to death. It's probably greater than zero. Probably higher here in Providence than it would be in Little Penwick. But it happens. Luckily, it didn't happen to you the other day. Because my son saddled up, came up here and took care of business."

He paused. Let her think about that.

"He did that for two reasons," Julius continued. "One, because he loves you and you were in danger. But two, he did that because there was nothing else he could do. He's a cop. You were in trouble. He came and rescued you. Sure, there was risk involved. Could have gone completely wrong. He coulda got shot. You coulda got shot. All the women you counsel coulda got shot. But none of them did because Junior used his training and his skill and his impetuous nature to walk into your place, where a guy was holding a gun to your head, and he took him down."

Miss Daisy brought out their plates. The chicken looked perfect. Smelled pretty good, too. Julius picked up his knife and fork and waved one across the table at Maggie.

"If it was me?" he said, "I'd be right proud of that man. Thankful that he exists. Grateful that he's my friend. And I'd probably want to spend the rest of my life ... as long or as short as the Good Lord decides that life will be ... spending every available minute with him."

He cut a big piece of chicken off the bone, scooped some slaw on top of it and forked it into his mouth. Where it practically melted.

"But I'm just an old coot, retired, over the hill and out to lunch," he said. "You'll have to decide for yourself what you want to do. And we'll all support you, whatever you decide. Because we like you and we think you're a special person." He stopped and ate some more.

"But you'll never be alone in any of this," he said. "You're part of a family, and not just me and Gus and Siggi and that little dumpling in there …" He pointed his fork at her belly. "Your family will also include everyone in uniform. Little Penwick, Rhode Island, Massachusetts. Doesn't matter. You'll be part of the deal. Supported, cherished, protected, loved. Never alone. So keep that in mind, too."

Maggie was finding it hard to eat. She pushed some food around her plate while she thought of what Julius was saying. Her eyes watered, her lips quivered.

"I appreciate all that, Julius," she said finally. "I really do. I just don't know …"

"S'OK, kid," he said. "You'll figure it out. It's only life."

CHAPTER 26

You always gotta have a Plan B. Fact of life. Things don't always go according to Plan A. You always need a backup. Sometimes you need a backup to the backup.

So apparently, Gus Haddock found my money wherever Danny Ferro hid it last fall. Ricardo's man saw it at the police station. He went down there to get some papers signed for Ricky's Fourth of July party at this old rocker guy's place on the river down there … and the stupid cops opened the safe and he saw the cash in there.

So it's on to Plan B.

No, I'm not gonna charge into the police station with guns a'blazin' and demand my money back. I might be a lot of things, but suicidal ain't one of 'em. I'm smarter than that.

It'll take a little finesse. Maybe some head knocking. Hopefully nothing more serious than that. But that's up to Chief Haddock and his merry band of idiots. He'll fork over the money. Or else. And I'm not gonna say what the 'else' is. Let's just say it won't be pretty.

The only trouble with Plan B is that I gotta depend on Ricky. I don't like depending on other people for stuff I want to do. They always want something back in return. Usually a good cut of your cash. Sometimes more.

Ricardo wants the more part. No doubt about that. He's told me that he wants me in his bed. I always remind him that he has a wife and that she wouldn't be real happy to hear that he is stepping out on her. And he knows I'd tell. Because I said so, many times. It's worked, so far. But he still wants me. I can see it in his eyes. The way he looks at me. I can read his mind. I don't know why I even bother wearing clothes when I'm around him. He doesn't see clothes when he looks at me. Creepy. To the max. But then, he's a man. They're pretty much all like that.

Speaking of Plan B, Ricardo himself is going through one. Apparently the gangster business is changing. Big time. Think about it. Years ago, guys like Ricky were into all kinds of things: prostitution, drugs, gambling, moving black market goods around to sell without having to cut the government its taxes.

Look at things today: nobody needs prostitutes anymore. Just go online and you can look at millions of naked women doing anything and everything. For free. Even Ricky's chain of strip clubs has seen business drop by half or more. Drugs? Half the stuff they used to sell is legal. People walk around in public smoking weed ... big deal, right? Everyone expects that the rest of the stuff will be legal too, sooner or later. Not much profit in trying to sell stuff you can buy cheap at the local Cumberland Farms, right?

Gambling? It's all legal and online. Nobody calls their local bookie anymore. He only takes cash and will break your leg if you fall behind. Now, there's a goddam casino or sports book on almost every corner, plus all the online gambling sites ... all legal and above board. And they take your credit card. If you get behind, you get a sternly worded letter from an attorney. Ooo, how scary is that?

And the black market stuff? Ricky used to have a pretty good business selling black market cigarettes, cutting out the middleman, the state. Plus all the stuff that used to fall off trucks and all. Not as much of that going on these days. You can buy whatever you want on EBay or Craig's List. Low prices, too. Maybe a lot of that stuff is stolen, but who cares? The Internet cuts out a lot of middlemen and Ricky Giancarlo is just a middleman. Steals from Person A, sells to Person B, takes his cut. Now, Person A and Person B meet on a chat line somewhere and do their own deal. Delivered by UPS! Sweet.

So that's why Ricky is moving into the music business. He thinks there's big money in controlling bands, putting out records. I think he's dreaming, but I'm not gonna tell him that. I need him. If just for a little while, until I get my cash and vamoose. Those guys in Argentina are still waiting for me. The future awaits!

But first, I gotta get that cash from Gus Haddock. But I got a plan for that.

Plan B.

CHAPTER 27

THERE WAS SOME rain on the morning of the Fourth, but by mid-afternoon, the sun was out and it was muggy. Late in the afternoon, Gus drove over to Slate Evans mansion and parked in the tradesman's area behind the five-car garage that sat slightly apart from the main house. He looked over at his father, sitting in the passenger's seat.

"You ready?" he asked.

"I was born ready," Julius Haddock replied.

There was a lot of traffic coming and going. The caterer's van was parked near the kitchen entrance and next to that was a florist's truck, back doors open. There were three rather beat-up looking panel trucks parked in a row. Gus figured these held the band's gear for the concert: amps and lights and instruments.

Gus and his dad got out of his car. He was dressed in casual clothes, suitable for a rock 'n' roll party, except for the Sig Sauer he had tucked under his shirt behind his right hip. He looked at his father, similarly dressed and, Gus knew, also packing.

They walked over to the main house, checked in with a security type at the back door and made their way down to the basement. Next to the extensive kitchen, bustling with activity, they found John King's security office, in a small windowless room. King was on the telephone. His assistant, a guy named Kenny, the one Slate Evans liked to call 'Kong,' was sitting before a bank of computer screens that showed scenes from the security cameras positioned throughout the mansion and its grounds. Kong was wearing headphones and muttering things to unseen people on a wraparound mic.

King got off the phone. He looked up and nodded at Gus. "You guys ready for the big show?" he asked. He stood up and extended a hand out to Julius. "You must be the father. I understand you're a big Slayers fan."

"Been listening to them since before you were born, sonny," Julius said. "Saw them back in '72, live at the old Schaeffer Stadium. You probably don't remember that place. Before your time."

Gus was looking at Kong's bank of screens. "How many men you have tonight?" he asked.

"Ten," King said. "Four in the parking areas, five in and around the grounds, one down by the dock."

"When does Slate get here?" he asked.

"He's already here," said a voice from the door. They all turned to see Slate Evans standing there. He was wearing a silk shirt with fluffy arms and lacey lapels, and a pair of black pants in a stretchy fabric that hugged his legs. The bandana holding his wild hair in place was the same color as his shirt. Gus noted that he had put on some stage make-up and outlined his eyes with kohl.

"Evening, Chief Haddock," Slate said. "Good to see you again."

"You two know each other?" King said, sounding surprised.

"Old and dear friends," Slate said, smiling at Gus. He turned to Julius. "Mr. Haddock, senior," he said, "Welcome to the party, sir. So glad you could make it."

"Thanks for having us," Julius said. "Looking forward to hearing you play."

Gus turned back to King. "We'll get out of your way," he said. "When do the guests start arriving?"

"Gates open at seven," King said. "Music starts at eight-thirty. Fireworks an hour later. Give or take."

"Come, gentlemen," Slate said. "Let's go see if we can score some liquid refreshment."

Evans led them past the kitchen, up a set of back stairs and through the central foyer into the back yard. There were people scurrying everywhere getting things ready for the party. The big sound stage, where the band would play, was set up on the upper patio level, facing back down toward the river. Long tables, covered with white tablecloths, were set up on the pool level and the catering staff was beginning to bring out trays of food for the buffet arrangement. The pool house had been transformed into the main bar for the evening, and a staff of a half dozen was preparing the set-ups, slicing lemons and limes, and stacking glasses.

"Dang," Julius said, taking it all in. "Big freakin' deal, isn't it?"

"Normally, I'd be wondering how much this is all costing," Slate said, looking around at the bevy of activity. "But then I remember, I'm not paying for all this. The record company is."

"Using your royalty money," Gus said.

"Oh, yeah," Slate said. "Wankers."

"You remember the drill?" Gus said to him.

Slate nodded. "We play for about thirty minutes," he said. "And then …"

"Duck," Julius said, reaching to pluck an hors d'oeuvre from the tray of a passing waiter. He plopped it into his mouth and smiled.

Slate looked at the elder Haddock. "You seem quite calm," he said. "How is that?"

Julius looked at Slate. "Sonny, I've been a cop for almost forty years," he said. "Not much surprises me anymore. I mean, you've been playing guitar for about that long. You still get nervous before a show?"

Slate smiled. "Used to throw up before going out on stage," he said. "Even when I was doing all those drugs. These days, naw. Just another bloody job, right?"

Just then, three young girls, all under the age of ten and dressed in flowing cotton dresses, came screeching up to Slate, crying out "PopPop! Grampy!" Their nanny, all in black, trailed after, smiling indulgently. Evans swept up all three in a huge hug.

"These three are my beautiful angel girls," he said to Gus and Julius. "What makes life worth living." He looked at Julius. "You have grandkids?"

Julius smiled. "No," he said. "Not yet." Gus shot him a look, but Julius was still looking at Slate's granddaughters and smiling at the scene.

"Are they going to be at the concert?" Gus asked. He was worried. He had a plan, but there was always a chance something might go wrong. In fact, not just a chance, but a strong likelihood.

"Naw, mate," Slate said. "They'll be watching from the windows of their room." He nodded up to the second floor. "In fact, I'm going to take these angels up to heaven right now. Get 'em settled in and ready."

He nodded at Gus and his father and led the girls back into the house.

They watched them go. "What now?" Julius asked.

"I need to check on the troops," Gus said. "Make sure everyone is ready."

"Already found one," Julius said. "She's helping to set up the bar."

Gus turned to look at the pool house and saw his second-in-command, Jessica Martin, behind the counter of the bar. She was dressed like the other servers from the catering company: black slacks, white shirt, black bow tie. Gus wondered where her gun was. She was dumping buckets of ice into a big cooler beneath the bar. Gus and Julius wandered down past the pool.

"Can I get a Long Island ice tea?" Julius said. "Extra ice and two cherries?"

"I'm sorry sir," Jessica said, "But we're not serving until …" She looked up and saw them standing there. She started to laugh, but remembered she was undercover. She quickly glanced around, but her co-workers were all busy with their tasks and not paying attention.

"Everything OK?" Gus asked her. Jessica nodded. "Can I keep the tips?" she asked. "Might make this evening financially worthwhile."

"It's a private party," Julius said. "Probably no tip jar."

"Oh, crap," she said.

"You seen Buzz?" Gus said.

"He was supposed to be working with the parking people," she said. "Haven't seen him in half an hour. But he'll get back up here when the music starts."

Gus nodded. Everyone was in place. They were ready. He hoped.

DUSK WAS BEGINNING to fall around eight. The backyard grounds at the Evans mansion were full of people. About half were milling around the pool, sipping cocktails and admiring the views. Others were lined up at the buffet, filling plastic plates and sitting down to eat at one of the dozen or so tables scattered at the far end of the patio. Still others were standing and gawking at the mansion that rose above the scene, a silent but imposing reminder of Slate Evans' wealth. The sound system was playing some of The Slayer's greatest hits.

There was a sound of a horn from down on the river, a deep, piercing single blast and most of the people at the party turned to look down the hill. A long, sleek motor yacht, shiny white with a three-level superstructure that featured black wraparound windows and topped with a flying bridge helm station, was gliding silently down the river and beginning to turn into a parallel position to the long jetty. Using the docking jets, the captain maneuvered the massive boat into position and brought her into the jetty. Two hands, fore and aft, tossed docking lines to men waiting on the jetty and the boat was quickly made fast.

Julius Haddock was watching. "You know how much fuel those things burn?" he said. "Around a hundred gallons an hour. My grandfather, J.E. Haddock, who was a commercial captain, would keel right over. But he was always a cheap bastard. Figures, since he lived through the Depression."

Once the boat was tied up, the people on board began filing off. A metal gangway had been extended out of a door on one of the upper decks, connecting with the jetty, and the people leaving the boat walked across it. They were all dressed elegantly. The women particularly wore dresses, short and long, while the men favored open neck dress shirts, nice pants and sockless loafers or boat shoes. Gus tried to do a head count, but eventually gave up. There were a lot of people on board. Most of them were still holding cocktail glasses of various sizes, but the group, after carefully walking down the long narrow jetty to land, made their way up the hill and gravitated to the pool house bar.

"You see Janine?" Gus asked his father, standing next to him. Julius was also watching the elegantly dressed guests wander down the long jetty heading towards the party.

"Not yet," he said. "She's not blond anymore, right?"

"Far as we know," Gus said. "But hair color is changeable." It appeared that all the guests on the yacht had embarked. Gus was also watching for Ricardo Giancarlo, figuring where he was, Janine Stone was likely to be nearby. He kept an eye on the gangplank and, sure enough, coming off the boat last were five huge men dressed in black suits and looking like they could each bench press five hundred pounds with one hand.

Once all five were standing on the jetty, one of them turned and motioned toward the boat.

Ricky Giancarlo came out next, followed by a young woman with jet black hair and a skin-tight full-length red dress slit up the side and plunging down the front. It was the Glitter Girl, Janine Stone.

"Black hair," Gus said to his father. "Got her?"

"You're looking at her *hair*?" Julius said. "Man, you need some lessons in oinky manhood. That's a pretty spectacular package right there."

They watched as the group — Giancarlo and Janine surrounded front and back by the five gorillas in the black suits— made their way slowly up the steps toward the pool level buffet area. Giancarlo stopped from time to time to shake hands with some man, and air-kiss the cheek of some woman along the way. He was the king of the walk tonight, and looked it.

Gus and Julius were standing off to the side on the pool level, next to the decorative stone wall that ran at knee level along the edge of the patio. They weren't hiding, but most of the people were crowded around the buffet table or standing in line to get a cocktail at the pool house, so they felt like they were mostly invisible to the other guests.

"Ladies and gentlemen," came a voice on the PA system, "Narragansett Talent is proud to present Slate Evans and his Friends!" Slate Evans led the way onto the stage, picking up his sleek Stratocaster guitar and striking some loud chords. "Evenin' folks," he said into one of the mics on the stage. "Happy July Fourth to one and all." The other musicians filed out after him: the bass player, another guitar, the drummer, three back-up singers and a small horn section of two trumpets and a trombone. The fans stopped eating and drinking long enough to cheer.

"We're just gonna play some old favorites for you tonight," Slate said. "And then we'll get out of the way and let you enjoy the fireworks." He turned to the others in the band. "Ready boys?" he said. The drummer started a rhythm with his kick drum and they launched into the opening chords of Believe Me, I'm Yours, one of the Slayers' most popular rockers. The drum, bass and rhythm guitar set the hard-charging beat, and Slate added a screaming solo riff high above before they segued into the first verse. Everyone in the audience began to sing along with the lyrics, since the song had been popular since the Slayer's hey-day in the Seventies.

Julius reached into his shirt pocket and pulled out two ear plugs, which he installed. He saw Gus looking at him and leaned over to get close to his son's ear over the thundering sound coming out of the huge amps onstage.

"Been going to rock concerts for fifty years now," he yelled. "Only reason I can still hear is because I've always used these."

Gus just nodded and smiled.

For the next thirty minutes, while the evening deepened as the sun sank slowly in the west, the band cycled through one Slayer's hit after another. Gus kept an eye on Slate and could see that he would often shoot a glance or a smile at one of the other musicians on the stage, probably for a wrong note or emphasis. Slate Evans had been playing these songs for decades, and could probably do them in his sleep. But the other guys were just trying to follow his lead and not screw up. Gus didn't hear any clunkers of wrong notes, but he figured Slate did.

The band played a little longer than originally planned and it was fifteen or twenty after nine when Slate held up a hand.

"Okay people," he announced. "The band and me-self are gonna take a little break here. I understand there are some fireworks on the menu. Enjoy!" He put his guitar down on its stand and led the band back off the stage.

Gus felt his pulse rate elevate. It was time. He looked at his father, who nodded, a smile playing on his lips. Julius seemed to be having a great time.

Giancarlo and his party had taken over one of the round tables on the edge of the pool patio. There were several bottles of champagne resting in ice baths. Gus and Julius walked over. Two of the five men-in-black bodyguards sidestepped and blocked their path. Gus and Julius stared at them. The gorillas stared back.

"*Lasciatemi dire passare*," Giancarlo said to his men. "Let them pass." He smiled up at Gus. "And a very good evening to you, gentlemen," he said. "Are you enjoying the band? Despite his years, Slate still has it, don't you think?"

"He's very melodic," Gus said. "As always. Needs his band mates, though. The guys you saddled him with are B-level, at best."

Giancarlo frowned. It was true, of course. But Ricardo was probably not used to people telling him the truth.

"What do you want," Giancarlo snapped. "I'm just trying to have a good time at the party. Don't need some small town cop bustin' my balls."

"Not your balls I'm here to bust," Gus said. He turned and smiled at the black-haired beauty by Giancarlo's side. "It's hers. Miss Stone, you are under arrest. Conspiracy to commit human trafficking, interstate transport of illegal aliens, evasion of a federal warrant and probably about six more things I got written down back at the station. Please step forward and put your hands behind your back." He flipped out his handcuffs that had been hiding on the belt under his shirt.

All five of Giancarlo's gorillas stepped forward. Gus and Julius were surrounded, cut off. Gus smiled. "Are you guys gonna aid and abet this fugitive from justice?" he said. "Damn, I hope you are. I think I can get all five of you hippos into one of my cells. Be fun to find out." He looked at Giancarlo. "Whaddya say, Ricky? You gonna make my Fourth explosive?"

One of the black clad men put his hand inside his jacket. He was staring at Gus.

"Wouldn't do that, Jack," said a voice behind Giancarlo. Everyone turned their heads. It was Buzz Franklin, still dressed in his caterer's uniform, standing in the ready position, gun drawn and leveled at the guy. Two of the other gorillas reached inside their jackets.

"Really would not suggest you do that," said another voice. All the heads turned the other way. Jessica Martin, black bow tie still in place, was holding her service revolver, also in the aiming position. When their heads turned back, Julius Haddock had his weapon in his hand, held down at his side.

Gus felt some of the guests standing nearby back away. There was an uptake of breath from everyone. Gus jangled the cuffs. "You don't want to start a bloodbath at your party,

Ricky," he said. "Probably put a crimp in your new music business. C'mon, Janine, let's do this the easy way. Game's over. You lose."

Through it all, Janine Stone had stood there, ramrod straight, only her eyes moving back and forth between Gus, Giancarlo, the gorillas and Gus' two officers on the flanks. Now she smiled.

"I'll go peacefully, Chief Haddock," she said. She walked up to him, twirled around and let Gus clip the cuffs on. Once he had her secured, he pulled out his cell and dialed.

"Situation contained," he said. "Bring in the backup."

Within seconds, everyone on the patio could hear the whoop-whoop of sirens. They sounded pretty close and that's because they were waiting out on the road outside Slate Evans' mansion. Six state police squad cars pulled through the gates and turned into the circular entrance drive that led to the front door. Another unmarked van pulled in behind, and a half dozen troopers dressed as if they were going to a SWAT party poured out of the back of the van, all carrying scary looking rifles and wearing full riot gear. They charged into the back of the house and began taking up positions on the various levels and stood in front of the sound stage.

Gus led Janine around the house and into the front drive. He walked her over to one of the state police vehicles and put her in the back of one. He leaned in and connected her seat belt.

"They'll take you to the women's intake," he told her. "I'll be up in a couple days, after the long weekend. We can chat

then. Happy Independence Day."
    She only stared at him as he slammed the door shut.

CHAPTER 28

THE NIGHT AFTER Slate Evan's July Fourth party, Gus and Maggie showed up for a cookout at Julius' house above the beach. Maggie had driven down from Providence that morning, and they had spent the day together, going for a swim at Crescent Beach and then back to Gus' apartment to shower and get ready for the evening. When they arrived, Julius' partner Siggi was busy in the kitchen preparing some of the food. Julius was outside on the deck, standing watch over his barbecue grill, monitoring the burning charcoal carefully, waiting for just the right moment to add the slabs of ribs to the fire.

Gus left Maggie inside to chat with Siggi and went outside to see if he could help. Or rather, to stand and talk with his father, who was always in complete command and control of the barbecue pit.

"Hey, Junior," his father said when he came outside. "Grab a brewski out of the cooler. Or if you'd rather, fix yourself a bourbon or something." Julius nodded at the various bottles and mixers set out on a side table at a corner of the deck.

Gus grabbed a beer and popped it open while he admired the view. The sun was low on the western horizon and the sky was turning some amazing shades of pink and orange. The changing colors turned the ocean into interesting shades as it washed fitfully up against the Rockies, that outcropping of boulders and islets that gathered just offshore from the beach below the deck. Gulls hovered high above, no doubt keeping an eye on the progress of the cooking about to happen down below, hoping that perhaps a tasty morsel of something might be tossed their way.

Julius was watching his son out of a corner of his eye, while he fussed with the coals.

"Good concert last night," he said. "A little short, though. If I had bought a ticket, I might be a little hacked off."

"Slate didn't want to play even that long," I said. "I talked him into starting the concert so that everyone would get into the flow of it. Figured it would be easier to confront her part way through."

Julius nodded, tipping back his own bottle of beer. "I would'a walked in, slapped the cuffs on her and shot anyone who got in the way," he said. "But you do it your way."

"I think it worked out OK in the end," Gus said.

"It was a nice collar," Julius said. "You got the lovely Miss Stone off the streets. At least until the lawyers spring her loose again."

"Should be a long while before she's walking the streets again," Gus said. "We've got four or five pretty serious counts on her. So far."

Julius nodded and tossed the two slabs of short ribs on the grill. They hissed and sent wisps of white smoke upwards.

Siggi and Maggie came out on the deck carrying bowls of salad, coleslaw, fries and a plate of cornbread, which they placed on the picnic table, which was set for four with colorful red, white and blue plates and napkins.

"We'll be ready in fifteen minutes," Julius announced, as he poked at the ribs with his pincers. "Seven and one-half minutes a side." He had a bowl of barbecue sauce and a brush with which he slathered the ribs with the sauce. The hissing and the smoke increased.

Maggie came over and peered at the grill. "Is that long enough?" she asked. "You can get trichinosis from under-cooked pork."

"Siggi brined these babies for a couple hours," Julius said. "Then she simmered them in boiling water for thirty minutes. I'm just adding the last layer of delicious with my sauce and the high heat. Been cooking ribs on the grill for forty years, Mags, and haven't lost a patient yet." He looked at her. "You want a beer? Glass of wine?"

Maggie smiled at him.

"I'm not drinking," she said. "Got a little Haddock passenger on board."

Siggi gasped when she heard that. Julius just grinned. Siggi went up to Maggie sweeping her up in a huge hug. Julius, having momentarily forgotten about his ribs, stared at the two women for a moment, and then turned to Gus.

"Son of a gun, sonny boy," he said. "That's pretty spectacular news. Congratulations!" He held out his hand for Gus to shake, but when Gus grabbed his hand, he pulled him close and gave him a hug.

"Wish you'd told us sooner," he said stepping back and looking at Gus. "I'd a bought some champagne to celebrate."

"Why don't you save that idea until the little one arrives," Maggie said. "Then I can join in."

Julius pointed his pincers at her. "I'll do that," he said, grinning. "You can make book on that."

Gus stood up and approached Maggie. He fumbled around in his pants pocket and came out with a small brown box. He flipped the lid open and handed it to her.

"This ring belonged to my great-grandmother, Vollie," he told her. "Obtained by John Edward Haddock, but no one in the family knows how he got it. It's long been a family mystery. Anyway, it would be an honor to welcome you to the Haddock family and I hope this ring will be a symbol of my love, and that of the people here, for you."

Maggie's hand went up to her heart and she reached out with the other for the ring. Her eyes were watery when she slipped it on her finger.

"It fits perfectly," she said. "How did you do that?"

Gus could only smile and shrug. Maggie threw her arms around him and they hugged.

"I guess that's a 'yes,'" Gus said. Maggie, crying now, could only nod.

For the next several minutes, Julius and Siggi grilled Maggie. When did she know? When did she tell Gus? What did he say? Had she told her parents yet? Gus sat on one of the benches at the picnic table and watched and listened. He felt at peace, for the first time in quite a while. He and Maggie had talked it all out. They had a plan. He felt like it was going to work out.

Gus thought about his grandfather, who he never really knew. And about his great-grandfather, J.E. Haddock, the man who had built this house. He thought about the generations of Haddocks, the ones who had come to this continent to forge a new life, and the ones who stayed behind in the old country. Generations, going back centuries, millennia, back to the misty beginnings of time. And one thing they all had in common is that at one time in their lives, they had gathered with their families, maybe over grilled meat of some kind, and announced that a new generation was about to be born. It was a time of excitement, and joy, and hope for the future. A hope that the Haddock that was to come would find a world welcoming and warm and full of love.

"Ding ding ding," Julius finally said, poking again at his grill. "These bad boys are done and ready to be eaten. Let's do it!"

He put the ribs on a platter and separated them into individual pieces with a big knife. They all sat down, passed around the bowls of sides, and filled their plates. The sky in the east had darkened to a deep purple, and Gus thought he could see a star—or maybe a planet—winking down at them.

They had been eating for fifteen minutes or so—with lots of laughter and jibes and stories and advice—when they heard a knock at the front door.

"We're out back," Julius yelled. "Come around by the garage!"

Gus had just put two more of the juicy ribs on his plate and was adding a big spoon of cole slaw next to them, when a tall black-haired woman climbed the three steps leading up the deck. She was holding a gun in her right hand and pointing it at all of them.

"Hi folks," Janine Stone said. "Got enough for one more?"

Instinctively, Gus reached for his Sig Sauer in the holster on his right hip. Janine saw him.

"Uh-uh," she said, shaking her head sternly and pointing her gun at him. "Let's not start our party off with a bang," she said. "That goes for you, too, chief." She looked at Julius, who was calmly munching on a rib, fingers greasy. He looked up at Janine, smiled a greasy little smile and kept eating.

Gus put his hands back on the table. Maggie was sitting to his right. He began thinking of ways he could shield her if Janine started shooting.

"I thought you were in custody," he said. "You were when I left the party last night."

Janine smiled at him. "Oh, you big lug," she said. "Ricky has about half of the state police in his back pocket. You should know that by now. I was out of the lockup by midnight. Didn't even have to touch anyone's pee-pee."

Julius muffled a snicker while he chewed on a rib bone.

"What do you want, Janine?" Gus said.

"A very good question, Chief Gus," she said, smiling down at him. "The answer is pretty simple. I want my money."

"What money is that?" Gus asked.

"Don't play dumb," she snapped. "You know exactly what I'm talking about. Because you already took my money out of the box Danny Ferro put down the well. Now, you're going to get it and give it back to me."

Gus chuckled. "Miss Stone, I have no idea what you're talking about."

Janine turned and fired a bullet into a red clay flower pot in which Siggi had planted a red geranium plant. They all flinched at the sound of the shot, which was followed by the pot exploding into shards and dirt.

"Cut the crap, Haddock," she snapped. "I don't have time for your bull. You've got my cash and I want it back. Now."

"OK, OK," Gus held up his hands as if in surrender. "I hear you. Why don't you sit down? Are you hungry? Have some dinner. Let's talk about this."

Janine walked over to the table and stuck her pistol against Maggie's forehead.

"I'm not hungry, I don't want to sit down. I want my money. You've got ten seconds to get your ass going, or I'll blow this lovely little lady's brains all over this deck."

"Don't do that," Julius said, wiping his greasy hands on a paper napkin. "I just re-stained this deck a few months ago. Hate to have bloodstains ruin the job. Takes a lot of work to clean up blood, y'know."

Janine looked at him, her eyes questioning. "Shut up, old man," she said. "I'm talking to the chief."

Julius shrugged. "Just sayin'," he said.

"Look, Miss Stone ... Janine," Gus said. "We got the money in the safe at the station house. It's in Jessica Martin's office, and I don't know the combination. It's the Fourth weekend, everyone is home having cookouts, like us, and it will take me some time to find anyone and have them come in and open the safe. So you might as well sit down and relax. This is gonna take a while."

"Just do it," Janine hissed. "IF I don't have my money in hand in one hour, I'm going to start killing the women at this table. Starting with this one." She shoved the barrel of her pistol further against Maggie's forehead, causing her to shrink back. Her eyes were wide with fright.

"OK," Gus said. "My phone is in my back pocket. Next to my gun. I'm going to get it out, OK?"

"Wait!" Janine said. She stepped over behind Gus and took his gun out of his holster. She carried it over to a side table against the deck rails and laid it down. Then she looked at Gus. "Okay," she said.

Gus pulled out his phone and dialed the number for the station. Dottie Adams, the dispatcher, answered. Gus couldn't remember a time when she hadn't been at the station to answer his call.

"Little Penwick Police," she said. "How can I be of service?"

"Hey Dottie," Gus said, trying to keep his voice level and free of stress. "Can you please call Lt. Martin and ask her to come in?"

"Sure, Chief," Dottie said. "Whaddya need?"

"I need her to open the safe and bring the contents over to Julius' house," he said. "As soon as possible, please."

"Wait, what?" Dottie said. "You know the safe is in Buzz' office, not Jessica. And it's got all that money from the box in the well. You want her to bring that to Julius' house? What for?"

"Don't ask a lot of questions, Adams," Gus said, trying to sound angry. "It's important that you get this done right away."

He hung up the phone abruptly. He looked up at Janine. "Taken care of," he said. "I figure maybe an hour, two at the outside. You sure you don't want something to eat while you're waiting?"

Gus knew that Dottie would stew about the conversation he had just had. She would know something was wrong. He never called her Adams. And she was smart enough to realize that bringing the contents of an evidence safe to some non-official location, even if it was the home of the former chief of police, was highly irregular. Gus hoped that she would wonder what the hell was going on and call either Jessica or Buzz and ask what to do. One of those officers would understand that something was wrong and send someone to Julius' home to investigate. Or come themselves, if they were available.

"You sure you don't want anything, hon?" Julius asked Janine. "It's all pretty good, if I do say so myself. My barbecue sauce recipe is a closely guarded secret."

"I don't want your food," Janine said. But she looked down at the remains of the meal. And she couldn't help herself. She hadn't eaten in several hours. She reached over and grabbed a square of cornbread and popped it in her mouth.

"Would you like a beer?" Julius asked, smiling at the woman. "Nice and cold."

"Shut up, old man," she snapped.

Siggi stood up suddenly. Janine swung her gun around and pointed it at her. Siggi raised her hands.

"Don't shoot!" she said, her voice thin and nervous sounding. "I have to pee." She nodded at the house, her eyes looking desperate.

Janine looked at the older woman, appraising the situation. Then she nodded.

"You got exactly two minutes," she said. "If you're not back out here, I'll shoot the old guy." She pointed her gun at Julius, who sat with his arms crossed, smiling calmly up at her.

"Never knew a woman who could get in and out of the john in less than five minutes," he said. "Try and hurry, Sig. Sox have a series with the Yankees next weekend and I'm looking forward to watching it."

"You old fool," Siggi said, and gave Julius a quick peck on the forehead. Then she hurried inside.

"How are you gonna pull this off, Janine?" Gus asked. He was trying to count off the seconds in his head. He might have to take some action if Siggi didn't make it back before the deadline. "Even if you get away from Little Penwick, there will be all kinds of alerts and BOLOs and APBs. They'll be watching all the airports, train stations. I don't see how you can get away. Be better if you gave me that gun and we can work something out."

"Shut up," she hissed. "I have a plan. You'll never find me."

Gus shrugged, pretending to be nonchalant. "Okay," he said. "We'll see."

"You're damn right we'll see," she said. "You'll see what an insignificant, crappy little cop you are in this crappy little town. They'll be talking about how you let a girl get the better of you three times. You'll be a laughing stock."

The screen door popped open and Siggi came back onto the deck, wiping her hands clean with a paper towel. Janine glanced at her and waved for her to return to her place at the picnic table, next to Julius. Then she turned back to Gus. She had more to say.

So she didn't notice when Siggi walked past the small table where Janine had laid Gus' gun down. Without breaking stride, Siggi picked up the gun, pointed it at Janine and pulled the trigger. The gun barked loudly. The shot went into Janine's right shoulder. She yelled in pain and dropped her gun as she fell to her knees. Gus leaped up and kicked the gun away. Janine fell forward onto the deck and groaned.

Julius rose slowly from the table and came to stand over Janine's prostate body.

"Dammit it all," he said, "I told you not to bleed on my deck."

Gus went over and hugged Maggie. She was shaking. But she looked up at him and smiled.

"I guess I've signed up for a lifetime of gunplay with you Haddocks," she said. "God help me."

Gus turned to Siggi, who was standing in the same place, immobilized. She stared down at Janine, who groaned again.

"Nice shooting," Gus said to Siggi. "Where'd you learn to do that?"

Siggi moved her eyes away from Janine to look at Gus. "I think one of our first dates was when your father took me to the shooting range," she said. "He's taken me shooting since then, hundreds of times. He used to tell me I was a better shot than him."

Gus carefully took his weapon out of her hand. "Looks like he was right," he said. He picked up his phone and started to dial the emergency number. Then he stopped.

All four of them heard the faint sound of sirens in the distance, growing louder.

CHAPTER 29

It was a beautiful October morning. Gus was working to get the final forms in place for the concrete truck that was due in an hour. The wooden forms rose from the bottom of the basement that Gus had excavated in the middle of his new two-acre lot on a small rise above Niwosauket Pond. It was a native word meaning "place of two brooks." Gus was checking the connections, to make sure the walls of his basement foundation would be straight and true.

Maggie sat in the shade of a stand of cedar trees that grew off to one side in what would soon be their front yard. Her belly was round and extended: the baby was due in another six weeks. She was listening to music on her headphones and sipping at some iced tea. She looked over at Gus and smiled.

A car turned onto the dirt tracks that served as the driveway for now, pulled up and stopped and Julius Haddock and Siggi got out. Siggi went back to the trunk and pulled out a wicker picnic basket. Maggie stood up and came over to help set up the lunch. Julius ignored all that and jumped down into the basement and examined the connections on the forms.

"They got this down to a science, don't they?" he asked his son, shaking the forms that were set to create a solid ten-inch-thick foundation wall.

"Pretty much," Gus nodded. "Once the concrete cures, we can start with the carpentry."

"How long you think until it's finished?" Julius asked.

Gus shrugged. "I've lined up a lot of help," he said. "If we get some breaks with the weather, I think we'll be pretty much finished by the first of December. That'll give Mags a month or so to move in furniture and all, and get the nursery ready."

"Sounds about right," Julius nodded. "I'll be over as much as I can."

"Unless you pick up an interesting new case or something," Gus said.

"Well, of course," his father said. "A man's gotta eat, after all."

"Lunch is ready!" Siggi called. She had spread a blanket in the shade of the cedars and unpacked sandwiches, chips, cold drinks and a plate of brownies.

"What have you heard on the Stone case?" Julius asked as they helped each other climb out of the basement.

"Not much," Gus said, dusting himself off. "The feds snapped her up after she was released from the hospital and took her off somewhere. She's facing about ten counts of trafficking and a few other things, so I expect she'll be inside for a long time."

"Excellent," Julius said. "That's one of the few good things about the feds. They take your perp away, but you never have to worry about her again."

"I'm just hoping that neither Janine or Ricardo has any pull with the U.S. Attorney or the Marshal service," Gus said. "Don't want to see her walking up my driveway any time soon."

There was a cheerful honk as one of the Little Penwick squad cars pulled onto the dirt track and stopped behind Julius' car. The doors opened and Jessica Martin got out of the driver's side, and LaToya Crenshaw from the passenger seat. Both were dressed in their uniforms. Within seconds, another car arrived, this one an unmarked car. Buzz Franklin was driving, and he had two people as passengers: Cassie Williams and Dan Jackson. All three were dressed casually.

More food came out of both of the newly arrived cars, and pretty soon, there was an official picnic going on under the cedars. The men stood around talking, while the women sat on a blanket that had appeared from the trunk of someone's car.

Gus turned to his father. "Actually, the really good thing about the feds is that they have a law saying the town can keep any recovered monies that were used for illegal activity. Thanks to Janine and her box of money, the town was able to offer positions to three new candidates, instead of just two."

"Better watch it, son," Julius said. "Based on the size of your force, people'll start calling Little Penwick a mid-sized town."

Gus chuckled. "We might have to expand the Town Council from five to seven members," he said. "Maybe you can run for a seat."

"I'd rather you just shoot me," Julius said. "Be easier for everybody."

He looked at the group enjoying the warm October sun and the picnic. "Think the people of this town will go along with your new hires?"

"I think so," Gus said. "They're all good people. I just need to turn them into good cops."

Julius nodded. "Anybody can do that, it's you, Junior," he said.

Maggie called out to Gus from under the tree. "Honey? Come sit and have some lunch."

"Be right there," he said.

Buzz Franklin had wandered over to stand in what would be the back yard of the Haddock house. He was admiring the view across the pond, which was achingly blue on this cloudless day. The leaves on the trees growing here and there around the pond were turning gold and red, and the colors glistened in their reflection on the water.

"How'd you find this place?" Buzz asked as Gus came up beside him. "What a view!"

"Helen Almy had a client, Betsy Schneider," Gus said. "Her husband passed about a year ago and Betsy was selling off their summer home down here. Turns out, she also had this parcel that old man Schneider had bought forty years ago. Helen told her that I was looking for some land to build on and she gave me a pretty good price."

"And you're still planning to build most of it yourself?"

Gus nodded. "My great-grandfather built his own place, down there on the beach," he said. "I thought that building my own place, something Maggie and I —and the kid—would love living in, was the way to go. Haddock family tradition and all that."

"I get it," Buzz said. "And you're going to have enough bedrooms in case the kid ever gets a brother or sister, right?"

"At least one," Gus said, smiling. "Any more than two will have to live in the barn."

"What barn?" Buzz asked.

Gus smiled. "Exactly."

When they got back to the picnic, Cassie Williams and LaToya Crenshaw were entertaining everyone with stories about their first few weeks on the job as probational officers in the Little Penwick police department.

"Oh my God," Cassie was saying. "After I wrote my first ticket for failure to yield, the guy looked at it and said 'I can't read this!' It was true! My hand was shaking so much, it looked like Arabic!"

"My first stop was just to warn a lady that she hadn't come to a complete stop at a stop sign," LaToya said. "She kept asking me 'Are you really a police officer in this town?'" She laughed at the memory. "I mean, she must have asked me that six times! I was riding with Officer Benes and he finally came over and told the woman that, yes, I was an official police officer. Too funny."

Gus listened to the story and made a mental note to ask Freddie Benes who the woman had been. He expected there would be some push back from some people in town to his new hires: two were black and two women. He wanted to stay ahead of it, if he could. Even Bob Murtha, the council president, had done everything except ask Gus outright if he had lost his mind. But Gus was happy with his new hires. They were bright, they were creative, and they all tried hard to learn the ropes. They all seemed to get what it meant to be a police officer. It was early yet, but he was confident all three would become excellent police officers.

"So what are you going to do now, Chief?" Siggi asked Gus. "Now that Janine Stone is off the board, there aren't any big cases left to solve."

Gus looked at his father's partner. She had been, and remained, remarkably calm about shooting Janine. It was like she thought it no different than any other household chore. Make the dinner, take out the trash, shoot the psychopathic armed woman who threatened them all. Ho-hum. Underneath, Gus thought that Siggi must have been churning with emotion. Staying up nights worrying. Hitting the bottle. Freaking out in some way.

But Julius had assured his son that Siggi remained dispassionate about the incident. "I trained her how to shoot," he said. "Told her about the circumstances when a shooting is justified. Explained how in those circumstances, shooting the bad guy is far preferable to letting the bad guy shoot you or a bunch of other people. So she just did what I had told her to do. No, she doesn't feel bad about it. Why should she?"

So Gus looked at Siggi now and smiled. "I'm going to police my town," he told her. "It's nice when there isn't anything major to take care of. But there probably will be, someday. So our job …"

He looked at the three new recruits and made sure they were listening … "Is to go out there everyday and be ready for whatever comes. Because something will, sure as hell."

"Amen," his father said.

ABOUT THE AUTHOR

James Y. Bartlett is an award-winning American novelist who has published 16 novels after a long career as a prolific magazine writer and editor.

His epic historical novel *Year of the Sheep*, set in the Scottish Highlands during the Clearances, was shortlisted in the 2021 Fiction of the Year contest by BookLife, the independent publishing industry magazine from Publisher's Weekly.

He has also written popular novels set in the world of professional golf in his *Hacker Golf Mystery* series; and about small-town cops in the *Swamp Yankee Mystery* series. He has also published six nonfiction books in his career.

Bartlett lives in a small town in Rhode Island.

For more information about the author and his books, please visit his website at:

www.jamesybartlett.com

The Hacker Golf Mystery Series

Death is a Two-Stroke Penalty
Death from the Ladies Tee
Death at the Member-Guest
Death in a Green Jacket
Death from the Claret Jug
An Open Case of Death
P.G.A. Spells Death

The last four titles are collected in a box set e-book edition titled "The Majors Collection"

The Swamp Yankee Mystery Series

Glitter Girl
Cold Secrets
Rainbow's End
Family Affairs
Rum Row*

* *A Prequel/Novella available in e-book format only*

The Bach Musical Mystery Series

The Organ Job
The Coffee Garden
The Song of Asaph

Also available in German translation

Historical Fiction

YEAR OF THE SHEEP: A NOVEL OF THE
HIGHLAND CLEARANCES

Other titles by the author:

CADDIEWAMPUS: LOOPING FOR GOLF'S GREATS
SERPENT POINT: A POLITICAL THRILLER*
THINK LIKE A CADDIE/ PLAY LIKE A PRO
MASTERING GOLF'S TOUGHEST SHOTS

Published under the pseudonym Caleb Clarke

Enjoy a Preview

FAMILY AFFAIRS
A SWAMP YANKEE MYSTERY
BOOK FOUR

In this exciting new adventure, Preston Knox, the corrupt Rhode Island Attorney General introduced in *Glitter Girl*, the first Swamp Yankee mystery, is found murdered in his home, just months before the election for Governor he was sure to win.

The prime suspect is none other than Julius Haddock, retired police chief in the town of Little Penwick, who had a history with Knox. But the suspect turns into sleuth as the sitting Governor appoints Julius to the investigation team to search for Knox's killer. One by one, the team finds and elminates suspects, until there's only one left. Meanwhile, Julius has to deal with other mysteries and problems a little closer to home.

Read the first chapter of James Y. Bartlett's thrilling new novel. To be notified when Bartlett's next book goes on sale, please visit www.jamesybartlett.com and join the mailing list.

CHAPTER 1

I WAS ENJOYING the warm sun of an early October afternoon on the deck behind my house. Here in southern New England, we have more than our fair share of crappy weather. Enough to make many of us cranky much of the year. From December through March, and sometimes a little more on either end, we are subject to blizzards, ice storms, or cold sideways rain. Sure, we all have our L.L. Bean flannel shirts and fuzzy-flap lumberjack's hats and lined gloves and mittens and thick woolly socks … but winter in New England can be cold and damp and unpleasant.

March and April are the heartbreakers: there are hints that the long cold winter of our discontent has passed, but those brief hints are followed by more cold, more snow, more freezing. July and August can be scorchers, with high heat and humidity making summer life entirely unpleasant; and September can be a reverse heartbreaker, with hints of cool fall followed by another week in the 90s.

But October's weather, which sometimes lasts well into early November … now those are the weeks we love around here. That big ole ocean out there finally gets to its peak warm temperatures in August and holds onto that warmth until the first freeze. Warm ocean means warm air. So even as the days get shorter and the trees start to turn colors, October is usually close to perfect: warm sunny days and clear cool nights good for sleeping with the windows open and a light blanket on the bed. Unless a hurricane blows up from the tropics, we get perfect football weather. Or late-season baseball weather. Or for the kids in high school, great weather for soccer and cross-country. Also great weather for golf, tennis, boating, fishing, cleaning up the garden, washing the car, doing a little painting or fix-up around the house. Don't need the heater, don't need the air conditioning. Just 30 or so perfect weather days.

So I was enjoying one, reading a book, sipping from a tall glass of iced tea and occasionally looking out at the Rockies, that collection of rocky islets and barnacle-covered boulders that lay just offshore of my beachfront home, around and through which the tides flowed happily, sparkles from the golden sun dancing atop the waves as they lapped on the rocky surfaces and the beach.

I had given myself permission to take the afternoon off. I'm retired, remember? My part-time private eye business had surprisingly been keeping me pretty busy over the last few months. When I helped my son, the current chief of police in our little Rhode Island town of Little Penwick, solve a 30-year-old cold case a few months back, I got my name in the paper. And that helped get the phone to ring. I now had three local law firms, one here in town and two more over in Newport, put me on the list of people they called for help to track down skip tracers, research insurance claimants and even do a couple of domestics. Those aren't my favorites — the world is an unhappy enough place without me having to follow around one spouse or another to see if they're doing the afternoon delight thing, and with whom — but the money is pretty good.

And in between times, I had been helping my son Gus build his new house, over near Niwosauket Pond. We had the foundations poured, the first-floor studs were up and work was moving right along. Right on schedule for the January appearance of Gus and Maggie's first child, a blessed event we were all looking forward to. Of course, Gus was pretty busy being chief of police, even though Little Penwick is not exactly a town rife with crime. I should know, since I had been chief of the department for twenty-four years, plus another ten as an officer on the force. While we occasionally had some bad crimes here — that 30-year-old Donna Dixon case had been one — most of the time life was pretty calm around here.

Siggi, my significant other, was working this afternoon at Dr. Harley's pediatrician office near the village green, and she'd be over later for dinner. So I was chilling out on the deck, working my way slowly through Howard Zinn's *A People's History of the United States*. I'd never gotten around to reading it before — it certainly wasn't on the reading list of the police academy when I went through there fifty years ago. But I thought it was about time, since Zinn was one of the first of the latter-day historians who decided to take an entirely new look at our historical record, this time through the lens of his classest, Marxist, anti-capitalist beliefs. You could draw a straight line between Zinn and people like Ibram X. Kendi and Nicole Hannah-Jones and the Critical Race theorists that had so many people's panties wadded up these days.

I was following the part where Zinn was writing about the prehistoric Moundbuilders of the Ohio River valley and their egalitarian culture, when I caught a movement in the corner of my eye at the fence on the far end of the deck. I glanced up and saw the head of a boy. He looked to be about twelve or thirteen or so. Tousled hair, brownish red, with a scattering of freckles across the forehead. He was staring at me over the top of the wall.

"Hey, there," I said. "Beautiful day, isn't it?"

His eyes widened slightly, but he said nothing.

"School out already?" I kept going. Mentally, I was trying to place him, but wasn't having any luck. I knew all my neighbors, and I didn't have that many, but couldn't think of any family nearby that had a pre-teen boy like this.

He didn't respond to that, either.

"You want some ice tea?" I said next. "I can scare you up a glass."

He smiled and shook his head. I wanted to pump my fist —Breakthrough! A reaction!!— but didn't.

"You're that cop," the boy said. His small dark eyes were fixated on me.

"Guilty," I said, putting the flap of the dust jacket in place and closing my book. "But I'm a retired cop now. Used to be the chief around here. Now my son is the chief." I looked up at him. He seemed to be following all that. "You need a cop, son?"

He blinked twice and then his head disappeared. When it didn't immediately reappear above my fence, I stood up and wandered over to the end of the deck. Looking back up towards the street from which my crushed oyster-shell driveway came down, I saw the kid climbing onto a bike, one of those with all-terrain dirt-bike tires and raked back handlebars.

"Hey!" I called out to him. He stopped, now athwart his bike and looked back at me. "You want to come back anytime, just come round the walkway between the house and the garage," I said. "I'm here most of the time. Knock on the back door. I'll keep the pitcher of tea cold for ya."

He smiled again, gave me a half-wave of acknowledgment, and rode away.

I DIDN'T THINK much about the boy after that. I went back to my book and chugged slowly through a couple more chapters. By then, my tea was gone and the sun was sinking fast into Aquidneck Island off to the west. I checked my watch and saw it was almost 4:30, so I figured I'd better get started on dinner. Siggi would be home soon, and after a long day chasing kids around the pediatrician's office, she'd be beat. I was planning some braised pork chops, along with some slaw from the head of red cabbage I had. Plus, I had a nice bottle of red from the local Sakonnet Vineyards in town, a blend of cab franc, merlot, and lemberger, a grape that did well in our local terroir.

I went inside, got the chops out of the fridge, washed and dried them and hit them with a lot of salt and pepper. I seared them with a little oil in a hot skillet and then put the chops and the skillet in a medium oven to roast away slowly for an hour or so. Then I got the cabbage out along with my big knife and was about to commence chopping when I heard Siggi's car pull down the driveway.

I stopped with the cabbage and opened the bottle of red. It needed to breathe a little and Siggi, after a quick shower and change of clothes, would be very ready for a glass.

Siggi didn't come in right away, which I thought idly was a little weird, but then she did. I turned to greet her with a smile, and saw the look on her face. The smile disappeared.

"Julius?" she said, voice wavering a bit. Her eyes were searching mine. Something was not right.

"What's the matter?" I asked.

"There's some men here," she said, "And ...'

Two large men came in the back door behind her. One was dressed in civilian clothes, a shirt and tie under a navy blue windbreaker jacket. The other was dressed in the full monty uniform of the Rhode Island State Police. He wore a gray jacket with flapped front pockets, a gray shirt and a dark grey tie, those absurd red-striped grey paints flared at the top that narrow down to stuff into the calf-height polished brown boots with a row of brass buttons down the front, and the round khaki-colored Stetson hats with the leather band and a nicely defined scoop depression in the front. Like a dimple in one's cheek. And, of course, the brown leather harness around the waist with the narrow leather strap up across the chest. It's a uniform that never fails to look great in a Fourth of July parade, but one in which I cannot imagine doing any kind of law enforcement in. At least, without falling down.

"Julius Haddock?" said the one dressed like a human being. The full monty trooper carefully edged Siggi out of the way. Just in case I went for my gun and started shooting. Which would be hard, since my firearm was in its holster hanging in my bedroom closet.

"Who wants to know?" I said. I know, a simple 'yes' would have sufficed. But they had just come crashing uninvited into my home, and I was not in the mood to be cooperative.

"We'd like you to come with us, please," the windbreaker guy said.

"Sure," I said. "Soon as you tell me why, where and what the hell is going on."

"We'd like you to answer some questions," windbreaker guy said. "Over at the Portsmouth barracks."

"Answer questions about what?"

"You are a person of interest," he said.

"I'm glad somebody finally noticed," I said. "But what case am I supposedly involved in?"

"Preston Knox," he said. Both of them gave me the stink eye. Waiting for me to begin shrieking and wailing 'I didn't do it, you got the wrong guy!'

Instead, I said "The attorney general? What about him?"

"He was murdered this morning," windbreaker guy said. "We want to talk to you about that."

Siggi caught her breath and her hand went involuntarily up to her throat. Both the staties noticed.

I had been holding the corkscrew and cork all this time. Now, I carefully laid it down on the counter. I looked at Siggi.

"Call Gus," I said. "Tell him to meet me over at the Portsmouth barracks."

She nodded, most of the color drained from her face. I smiled at her, reassuringly.

"No worries," I said. "Just call Gus. Oh, and the pork chops are in the oven. Take them out in about forty minutes." She nodded again. She was still ashen faced. I turned to the staties.

"OK," I said, "Let's go."

www.ingramcontent.com/pod-product-compliance
Lightning Source LLC
Chambersburg PA
CBHW071430200726

48294CB00002B/576